Brenna Lyons
Rites
⊕f Mating

Kegin Series #2

FIREBORN PUBLISHING COPYRIGHT

STATEMENT

Rites of Mating
Copyright © 2005/2009/2017 by Brenna Lyons
Print ISBN: 978-1-946004-84-0
Print Publication: March 2017

Cover Artist: Brenna Lyons
Photo Credit: 123rf
Editor: Kathryn Lively
Logo copyright © 2014 by Fireborn Publishing and
Allison Cassatta
Licensed material is being used for illustrative
purposes only. Any person depicted in the
licensed material is a model.

PUBLISHER

Glossary of Keen Terms

Used in the Book

NOTE: Keen is a lyrical language, and minor changes in pitch and inflection denote a slightly different word in the language. See next page for the Keen calendar.

Assurances— the presentation of a bloodied blade to an injured woman, offering proof that the guilty party has faced his punishment at your hand

Auguren— a disinfectant used in the paste with Felgren to sterilize skin and equipment, poisonous when ingested

Burgel— a small blue flower that blooms late in winter/early in spring as the last of the snow recedes

Choc— a soft, brown color

Cimmeg— a heavy spice like cinnamon and vanilla mixed that strengthens the blood and aids in healing

Dolgen— a yellow/orange scrubby plant which yields a powerful aphrodisiac; sucre sweet, it can be ingested in a tea; for the most powerful and immediate potency, it is mixed in oil and applied to genitalia

Eir— an evergreen tree that gives a thick sugary sap which is edible; often used in bottling fruits

Emi bead— a soft (consistency of amber) clear emerald green stone usually shaped into beads and used for decoration

Felgren— a light choc plant with antibiotic properties; can be ingested in a tea, used in a paste with Auguren to sterilize skin and equipment, and burned to create acidic fumes to ward off dangerous animals and enemies

Fion— Keen queen of the gods; Goddess of love,

balance, and mercy

Fion's Children/Daughters— The matriarchal priestess race wiped out by the Lengar in Ti 10-452

Garigol— a powerful sedative and muscle relaxant derived from the leaves of the tree of the same name; causes confusion and lethargy followed by sleep in higher doses; Jaglin crave it and will attack to steal stores of it, so it is stored in air-tight containers

Geela— a cliff-diving, carrion eating bird with gray and black feathers

Gelgrin— a confection made of Eir sap, lizor berries, implin, and cream

Gola— a plant that resembles mistletoe; its pink berries produce a poison that induces miscarriage and kills if left untreated; used to treat mother's sickness, it is treated with Triclum; a pernicious bush

Hi— prince, Your/His Highness

Hir— princess, Your/Her Highness

Hypocil— a metal pen-shaped device that injects medications through the dermis without an open site or risk of infection

Implin— a Kegin fruit akin to a Bosc pear; the core is a strong stimulant; the main ingredient in lover's repast

Iri— golden flowers that grow on vines as thick as a man's wrist; makes a soothing topical drug for use on rashes, minor burns and abrasions

Jaglin— large jaguar-like cats with thick black fur, dotted with gray spots as cubs

Kit— breeding cattle, which are used for food

Laes— Lady, noblewoman

Len— God of the underworld, vows broken, trickery, and havoc

Li— Lord, nobleman

Lizor— a fragrant purple flower whose berries make a calming tea, the stems make a powerful sedative to relax the mind and body, lizor is also used in forming a healing circle

Lover's Repast— the traditional cake of new lovers

and new mothers; Cimmeg and Implin cakes with warmed sucre sap served on the side

Maiden Bride— a tradition whereby a male may have the night before the contract signing with a bride believed virginal; if she proves virginal, by the blood on the sheets, her husband owes her father 500 gold coin at signing; if not, her father owes her husband that amount

Mag— Keen king of the gods; God of justice, law, and vows unbroken

Magden— the race ruled by Ro Ti in the days before unification

Magetra— Magistrate

Muklin— a plant akin to an Earth mushroom...small ones, the size of Portobello are stuffed and baked...larger ones are diced and fried or breaded and baked

Olum— a drug like an opiate that relaxes muscles, relieves pain, and suppresses the drive to vomit

Portrain— a boar-like creature found in the lower foothills of several mountain ranges

Regit Lus— (SEE Trial Moon)

Rig— queen, Your/Her Majesty

Ri— king, Your/His Majesty

Schaen— a male harem that, in ancient times, was kept for the use of royal females; named for the Schen.

Schen— the insatiable sex drive of a pregnant Keen woman

Schente— a harem of sterilized women kept for the use of royal men

Silin— a silk-like fabric that most women's clothing and royal bedding are made from

Stride— a measure of distance; the distance the average war-buck can travel at a loping stride (half-speed) in the space of five minutes

Sucre— a thick sugar syrup from Eir trees

Ti— conqueror, king who takes his land by force

Trial Moon— an ancient custom by which a Keen man may demand a contract by a woman he has had sex with, if certain conditions are met

Walla— a deep green wild herb that will act as a contraceptive when taken in a tea or used as a paste

Wariken— a large gray or deep choc furred beast which runs wild in packs in mountain areas; can be trained as a hunting beast or companion though always a bit wild

Zura— a gray bush; used in protection oils for blessing and healing circles; makes a tonic when mixed with Garigol that eases painful breathing

Keen Calendar

A year on Kegin is roughly equivalent to an Earth year. Days are twenty Earth hours long, but the year is separated into twelve months consisting of thirty-seven days each. A week on Kegin consists of eight of their days. I formatted the calendar as if the Keen year started in January like an Earth year. In reality, the Keen year begins in Endl. The end of winter and beginning of spring is a time of rebirth, and so it is the start of the Keen New Year.

Pri— January
Ite— February
Endl— March
Wos— April
Zor— May
Fim— June
Jad— July
Caj— August
Wend— September
Abrin— October
Veril— November
Iric— December

The Major Re-bred

Families of Kegin

Kell and Jenneane (Last Chance For Love 1):
Jole (Susan - Last Chance For Love 1)
Michael (Danellan - Last Chance For Love 1)

Jole and Susan:
Jenneane (Tirin - Rites of Mating 2)
Joseph (Berel - Rites of Mating 2)
Eve (Matchmaker's Misery 3)
Rebecca (Restrained 5)
Pyter (Restrained 5)

Michael and Danellan:
Gibril (Double Image 4)
Cro (Alien Encounters 6)
Kyra (Matchmaker's Misery 3)
Gandl (Restrained 5)
Dirin (Double Image 4)

Alex The Elder and Lyssa Braeden (Last Chance For Love 1):
Alex The Younger (Double Image 4)
Andrew (Double Image 4)
Pilar (Matchmaker's Misery 3)
Carter (Alien Encounters 6)

Jace and Jelise (In Her Ladyship's Service):
Cayce (Tale of Three Daughters 7)
Kylee (Tale of Three Daughters 7)
Kristee (Tale of Three Daughters 7)

DEDICATION

To Lisa, that one "twin" with which I click, and
Rob, the one person who makes life worth living
and brings passion to my life.

Author's Note

Welcome back to Kegin. I do apologize for the delay in this series, but I discovered that, since the last six books are so intertwined, I had to write large portions of further books in the series in order to have a firm handle on the characters, as they appear in *Rites of Mating*. I've learned the hard way with *Night Warriors* that I should never assume I know a character, until I have done an in-depth study into that character's mind. As such, I hesitate to give you half a look at a character, something that will become seriously flawed when I show him/her in a later book.

I hope you enjoy the next generation of Keen nobility. I know I am.

As always, there is a glossary of Keen terms used in this book.

Happy reading!

Brenna Lyons

Prologue

Preparation for a Bride

Pri 18th, Ri25-3007

The Earth-style celebration of Christmas

The schente giggled. "What are you doing, Highness?"

Joseph growled in frustration. If the schente found it amusing, he wasn't doing it right. He'd have to consult the text in his father's library which explained the ancient Keen seduction technique again. Learning the bel tro was essential. Joseph would have to win his bride, and Berel was worth nothing less than the rite of kings.

"Have I displeased you?" A touch of panic edged her voice. The schente *would* fear that.

Joseph had never admitted disappointment in a schente, even when it was true. The women had no greater prospects than a life of service or carrying cross-bred children, their genetics too shattered to make an advantageous marriage and produce viable children of their own. Joseph would never think of putting a woman out of service when it was obvious that they lived to fulfill their contracts.

He flopped onto his back, pulling the schente with him. "Never," he assured her, drawing her mouth to his.

The schente relaxed against his chest. Joseph

1

groaned as she worked her way down his body, taking his length in her mouth. He wound his hands in her hair, guiding her movements as she pleasured him.

Joseph closed his eyes, imagining another woman, the only woman he wanted but couldn't have—yet. Some days, Joseph wished he could turn the clock back a year to escape his adulthood, but the madness of adding another year to his waiting would not be worth the relief in other areas of his life.

He turned his mind back to Berel. Joseph was an adult, but Berel was still three years from that blessed day. Until then, the schente would be his only comfort.

Berel was in her sexual maturity. Joseph could take her with Walla teas, if she were willing, but Joseph wanted more than sex from Berel; and though lowborn could use the teas before their twentieth year, it wasn't suggested medically that they do so. He couldn't touch her and not take what he craved most from her. He knew himself that well.

The schente drove his body on. In his mind, it was Berel who teased his length with her tongue, Berel who sucked him deep into the wet heat of her mouth.

Joseph groaned. "Come on top of me," he breathed.

She swung a leg over, encasing him in a slice of the soul's reward. Joseph drove up into her, drinking in the scent of her arousal. It wasn't perfect. Berel would be virginal.

He tightened his grip on her hips. If Berel took

another before she was his, he would curse himself as a fool forever. If Joseph didn't wait for Berel, he would break laws in claiming her. If he lost her in waiting—

The schente squealed in delight as his thrusts became more fevered. A new understanding of how Michael could go insane for want of his mate seared him. Some nights, Joseph wasn't much better than his infamous uncle.

Her body contracted around him, and Joseph followed her over, filling her with seed that would find no purchase, locking into a band that would stimulate no egg for him. When he lessened, she left him as the rules stipulated she must.

Joseph lay on his bed for long moments, staring at the ceiling and listening to the heavy snow pelting the windows, alone as he always was when the schente left him. He bathed and dressed slowly, dreading the night to come.

He met Jenneane in the corridor. His older sister by a quarter hour looked as nervous as he felt.

"Ready for the crowds?" he asked.

She fussed with her gown. "Do I look ready?" she managed, her hands shaking.

Joseph squeezed her hand. "No. You look positively ill."

Jenneane smiled weakly, a smile that didn't light her green eyes. She wound her arm through his. It was a sign of solidarity, a promise that they would survive yet another night of being pawed and propositioned by the hopefuls. "I never could lie to you."

He led her down the main staircase and

through the entryway to the ballroom. The cheers started as they stepped through the doors. The nightmare started a moment later. Suitors pressed in—his on one side and hers on the other, all vying for their attention.

"A dance, Princess?"

Jenneane shook her head.

"Highness, my father is—"

Joseph shook the hand off his elbow.

"Princess Jenneane, my name—"

One of Panor's men pushed back a few suitors, giving Jenneane room to take a calming breath.

"I'm certified virginal, Prince Joseph."

Jenneane shot a startled look at the speaker, turning deep crimson at the lengths the suitors would go to. Joseph urged her on, ignoring that one with all of the other comments and offers thrown his way, sickened by the spectacle they made.

"Would you care for a walk in—"

Joseph dragged Jenneane to his side as the overbearing young lord grasped her arm and pulled her to a halt. He sent a warning scowl. The man fell back a step, and Panor's men stepped to the hopeful to hold him back. Joseph led Jenneane on, praying that the fervor would die down. The mob typically gentled, as the hours wore on. Tonight should be no different.

"The dais," she whispered.

Joseph nodded curtly and led the way to the seats set up for them at their parents' sides. It would mean only a momentary reprieve. The suitors dared not follow them onto the stage, but eventually Joseph and Jenneane would have to leave that safety and tend to their duty. They had to get to know the hopefuls and actively seek out one who would be a suitable mate.

He growled in frustration. *The hopefuls.* They were hopeful of little but the prestige of being chosen, of joining the ranks of the royals.

Their mother offered them weak grins as they settled into their seats. Susan hadn't intended this life for her children when she gave them life. She'd apologized for that more than once.

* * * *

Joseph bit back his rage. He reminded himself that his patience was worn thin by hours of dealing with grasping hopefuls. Still, he wasn't about to sit still for this.

Berel inched away from the noble who crowded her. Her smile was strained, and she flicked a glance at the dais.

He was on his feet and striding through the crowd without a coherent thought of why he was acting this way. Only one thought registered clearly in his mind. Berel was Joseph's, and no other man would touch her, especially one she so obviously didn't want.

Joseph brushed off the suitors with barely contained disdain. He would make it seem that he gave consideration, but unless Berel refused him, he wouldn't choose another. Joseph grimaced. She could refuse him. Despite the looks of interest Berel shot him, he might be misreading her intent.

Berel looked up as Joseph reached her side, gratitude in her eyes. "Joseph," she greeted him in a husky voice that sent tremors of pleasure through his gut.

Joseph smiled and offered his hand. "I believe you promised me this dance," he commented smoothly.

She took his hand and accompanied Joseph to the center of the floor without a backward glance at the upstart young lord who had been hounding her moments before. Joseph pulled Berel to his chest, then wrapped his hands around her waist, thankful that this was an Earth celebration with Earth-style dancing.

Berel wound her hands around his neck, her body pressed close to his. "Thank you for saving me," she breathed.

Joseph pushed back his anger again. "Any time. It gave me an excuse to dance with you."

She blushed, moving her body against his fluidly. "I love this song."

He nodded. It was a ballad from Earth, a traditional Christmas song, one of hundreds his mother had brought with her from her world.

Berel listened to the haunting tones. "Said the evening breeze to the tiny kit," she translated smoothly.

Joseph grinned. Her translation wasn't perfect, but it was nearly so. "*I love that you speak English.*" He offered the comment in English, thankful that he and Berel could be alone, even in a crowd.

"*How could I not? Being raised in a household that spoke it?*"

He took a calming breath, a thousand Earth endearments coming readily to mind. It was too early for that. Berel wouldn't be an adult for three years. When she was—Joseph hardened at the thought of claiming her.

Berel gasped, meeting his eyes in surprise.

Joseph offered her a sheepish grin. "*I am undeniably male, Berel. A beautiful woman in my arms...*"

She smiled, her eyes making offers she wasn't old enough to follow through on, her body brushing by his, firing him into a fierce state of arousal. He wasn't misreading her. Berel wanted him as desperately as Joseph wanted her.

The ballad ended and another commenced, a song about lovers curled before a fire while the snow mounted outside the windows. Visions of hanging a gola sprig over her and kissing every inch of Berel's body came unbidden, but not entirely unwelcome, to his mind.

"May I claim this dance, Highness?"

Joseph scowled at the lord over his shoulder, then at the lord's sister. He'd seen this treatment before. The lord would dance with Joseph's current partner, while his sister cornered Joseph.

"I'm sorry, Lord Byen, but I promised the lady to see her back to her family. Captain Tyrel is protective of his daughter."

Byen bowed, red-faced. "Of course, Highness."

Joseph threaded Berel's arm through his own and returned her to her parents with a warning to Tyrel to guard her from the more unscrupulous elements in the crowd. He took his leave, claiming fatigue. In truth, fatigue wasn't what Joseph felt.

He ached for Berel. His nerves were ragged.

"A schente," he barked at the guard who held position at the door to his rooms. There wasn't typically a need for guards in the royal chambers, but on celebration nights, things got crazy. Until the young royals chose their mates, it would be like this.

Joseph had stripped by the time the schente came to him. He had balked at the schente at first, accepting them only when he was told that the heir apparent would be expected to keep them. Joseph was glad that he'd agreed to the schente on nights like this. A willing woman he could momentarily relieve tension in might be the only thing keeping him sane for his chosen mate. *Berel.*

SECTION ONE:
Jenneane

Proof of a Maiden Bride

CHAPTER ⊕NE

Abrin 34th, Ri 25-3008

"Mother, I am not interested," Tirin Li, Captain in the royal guard, growled through clenched teeth.

Giriam Laes looked at him, paling at his scandalous words. "Not *interested*? It is your duty to make an advantageous marriage, Tirin."

He sighed, rubbing at the tight spot in his neck. It was a duty no one ever mentioned in the six years since adulthood, hoping that Tirin wouldn't find another and would win one of the re-bred princesses. Now that the princesses were coming of age, it was a duty he never heard the end of. "And I will do my duty, Mother. I am simply not interested in playing fawning fool to a pampered princess."

Tirin scowled at the throng of men surrounding the princess in question, begging for her attention, for a dance—or for more, if she were willing. The king's chief of security, Panor, pushed through the moving mass of male bodies and drew the young woman away to the angry chorus of the suitors. He scowled harder. *The hopefuls.*

It was disgusting. The men presumed too much. They looked at the princess. They touched her. Tirin fisted his hand as another reached out, and Princess Jenneane crowded closer to Panor to escape the grasping hands. By the laws of Kegin, it wasn't permitted. Soldiers should be forcing the suitors back, making them mind the laws.

Tirin kept his gaze respectfully lowered or averted, never looking directly at Princess Jenneane as she approached. Still, he glanced at her briefly out of the corner of his eye. Tirin bit back an expression of deeper disgust, settling instead for the same scowl. Her outfit was indecent, despite the current occasion.

The occasion was indecent enough. Many Keen nobles flocked to the Earth celebrations Susan Rig had introduced when her oldest children were infants. *Hallo-ween* was Jole Ri's favorite holiday, but it wasn't Tirin's.

Too many Keen reveled in the custom of wearing revealing costumes and going masked. Already, anonymous couples, drunk on iri brandy and lizor berry wine, were seeking darkened corridors for intimate encounters. Some of them wouldn't even know who they'd had sex with when the morning came.

Princess Jenneane's garment wasn't as revealing as some. It didn't show excess flesh. In fact, it hardly showed any, but it was snug to her body as if drawn on. A single garment of black silin covered her from above her ample breasts to ankle and wrist, leaving her shoulders completely bare. It hugged every curve and valley, leaving no secrets of the body beneath. Her boots were low, cuffed black hide creations almost as shiny as the silin. She wore a fur mask, the likeness of a jaglin, most likely done in real jaglin fur.

Tirin glanced again, drinking in the sight of her, heedless of the laws he was breaking, the laws he'd been supporting only moments earlier.

The princess seemed to glide across the floor, her hips swaying in a way that brought images of slow, deep kisses and hours of sex to mind.

His breathing hitched as he stared at her back full on. Her hair was a thick mass of choc waves with a rich under-cast of lizor berry burgundy that reached mid-curve on her buttocks, tangling around the base of the fake silin tail attached at the upper curve of her lovely backside. She was perfect.

Tirin muttered a curse. Princess Jenneane stopped, probably in response to his ridiculous outburst. He dropped his gaze as she turned back.

"I like your costume," she whispered, leaning close enough that her perfume teased his nose. It was a light scent, young iri blossoms like those that grew on the outside walls of the palace in late spring. It was feminine, alluring.

Tirin tried to bite back the smile curving his lips. *Costume indeed!* He was unmasked and wearing his guard uniform. He bowed slightly. "Thank you, Highness."

"Should I call you Captain, or do you prefer me to use a name?"

He forgot himself and his place for a moment and looked at her face. The princess's lips were pulled up in a wide grin, and her green eyes glittered in mischief. His eyes locked on the emi bead encrusted choker at her throat.

Tirin lowered his eyes again, pushing away an errant vision of leading Princess Jenneane to his bed by a leash on that choker. Dear Fion! Where had that idea come from? "As you wish, Highness," he managed.

"I'd—" She sighed. "I would prefer to use your name." The princess sounded uncertain, nothing of the self-assured temptress he'd viewed across the room.

"This is my son, Highness," his mother interrupted excitedly. "He is Tirin Li, son of my first mate, General Kyril."

Tirin felt his face heat. "Enough, Mother. My lineage is of no importance," he argued.

"Well, of course it is, dear child. Any prospective mate—"

"Mother, please."

"It's all right, Captain," the princess assured him. "I understand."

Before Tirin could gauge her sudden reserve, she was gone. His gaze followed her as Princess Jenneane left the ballroom. He growled in displeasure. More than once, she was forced to sidestep an overeager noble trying to lay hands on her.

Was this the life she led? Pursued? Men allowed to handle her, simply because she was of age to marry? Tirin hoped she chose a husband quickly and escaped this mockery of her purpose.

Or perhaps it wasn't that simple. After all, the princess sought out his company. She didn't seem overly vexed by the men crowding her. Perhaps she liked the attention. Tirin had heard as much bandied about in rumors he would like to believe were vicious lies.

He glanced at Princess Gibril in distaste. It wasn't as if the idea of a princess who enjoyed the games was a new one on Kegin.

"I think that went well," Giriam noted.

"Perhaps next time, you will offer more conversation for Her Highness's enjoyment, but she did notice you."

Tirin bit back a sound of disgust. It *had* been going well, until his mother interfered. "Why don't you go see how your daughter is progressing in her pursuit of Prince Joseph, Mother? I need a bit of fresh air."

He headed for the closest doors to the gardens without waiting for her answer. The last of the iri still in bloom sent visions of a silin-encased beauty with deep green eyes through his mind. Tirin pushed them away. He didn't want things to go well. Tirin didn't want a pampered princess.

Did he?

* * * *

Jenneane slipped into her rooms, sighing in relief. Every occasion for more than a year, state or holiday, had been like this. She could talk to her parents, but Jenneane feared what would happen if the soldiers felt compelled to enforce the mores with fight batons. No. It was better to endure the crowds of hopefuls and weed them down to someone she could accept as her husband.

She bit her lip, the memory of the captain she'd spoken to filling her mind. He'd endeavored to hold to the mores, though his arousal was painted in his deep choc eyes. There were no games with him, no posturing, and no bold advances. Were it not for Tirin's rather overbearing mother and the knot of suitors led by Lord Byen making their way toward her, Jenneane would have enjoyed continuing her conversation with him.

Captain Tirin was wonderful. His gaze was unassuming almost to the point of uncertainty. His face—Jenneane was glad Tirin wasn't masked as most of the other men were. He was tall and muscular like most Keen soldiers were, more than a full head taller than she was and beautifully male. His black hair was cut short in the manner of many of the younger soldiers, but still long enough to run fingers through. She wanted to see that face and body again, but how would she manage that without being mobbed?

Jenneane smiled, heading to one of her cabinets. The suitors would be looking for this ridiculous outfit that Eve designed for her. If she changed clothing, Jenneane could slip in and find Captain Tirin.

She stilled with her hand on a full-skirted green ball gown. What if Tirin wasn't interested?

"*Oh, be real,*" she grumbled in English. Was there a man on all of Kegin over the age of nineteen who didn't have his heart set on Jenneane's interest or the interest of one of the other princesses or re-bred ladies? "Probably not."

She pulled at the back closure of the costume in annoyance. It had taken Eve and Berel to get her into this bodysuit. Jenneane could call for a servant to help her with the tiny hooks, but that might take too long. She wanted to reach Captain Tirin before he decided to leave. Worse, any of her usual servants would see her nervousness, and she would be too closely watched to carry out her plan.

Jenneane unclipped the tail from the two tiny silin loops and tossed it aside. She'd have to wear the same mask, but the gown would cover her costume, and she could clip up her hair. Yes. That would do it. If she kept her gaze cast down, it would work.

A quarter of an hour later, she surveyed the results of her efforts. It was perfect. Now she just had to find Captain Tirin.

* * * *

Joseph smiled at the sight of the woman hurrying through the hidden corridors. Since he'd left the rest of his family in the ballroom only moments earlier, it had to be Neane. He hid in the ancient checkpoint designed to police the use of the corridors and waited for her to pass him.

He touched her shoulder, falling back with a laugh and blocking her blows. "It's me, Neanie. Calm down."

His twin sister struck him again with a frustrated growl. She really did hate people touching her without her consent. Joseph felt a pang of regret for causing her discomfort. She'd had more than her share in the ballroom.

"Are you insane?" she whispered in a fierce voice.

Joseph cupped his hands on her shoulders. "Come now. Who else would be in these corridors?"

Neane shook off his grip. "Why are you here?"

"I escaped just like you did. I'll bet Panor is furious with us."

"I don't particularly care."

"I know he's not Pyter—"

Neane scowled as she always did when someone mentioned their beloved 'Pappy.' "Don't compare them with me," she warned.

He looked at the ball gown, then the mask in her hand, his suspicion rising fast. "You've made your escape. Why are you going back in a new outfit?"

She shifted from foot to foot and pulled at a curl over her ear, a nervous habit she'd had for as long as Joseph could remember. "I— Oh, Joseph." Neane looked at him miserably.

He smiled. Neane wanted to lie, but she had never been able to lie to him. He glanced at the mask again, and his smile disappeared. "You're meeting someone, aren't you?"

"No." She glanced at his face, reading his mistrust clearly, just as he intended. "Not really. I'm looking for someone."

"Who?" he demanded.

"Please, Joseph. I just— I think I could like this one, if I could just get a few minutes of peace with him to find out. He doesn't hound me or paw at me." She looked heartbreakingly hopeful.

Joseph touched her cheek. "Father would gladly end that. You know he would if he knew how much it bothered you."

Neane shook her head. "Some fool would just get himself hurt."

"Better than them hurting you," he reasoned.

She lowered her gaze, pulling at the curl again. "No one has hurt me, Joseph."

Yet. But the crowds get more out of hand every time they gather. He sighed. "I'll take you."

"No," she gasped.

"Why?"

"You can't hide."

"Just to the ballroom. I'll leave you to find the man in peace."

Neane smiled in the dim light around them. "Thank you, Joseph."

"You still won't tell me who he is?"

"Soon. If he's the one. You have my word."

"Very well. I will probably hate myself for allowing this." Neane would be safe in the ballroom. Joseph could keep a close watch over her and intervene if the pack of suitors...or one suitor, in particular, got out of hand.

He led her through the corridors to the exit near the kitchens. They parted company there. Joseph laid a kiss on his twin's cheek, then pulled her mask over her face.

"Good luck to you, Neane," he whispered.

"And to you."

"I'll have Panor deflect the worst of the pawing. Don't be afraid to ask for help if you need it."

"I won't."

Joseph made his way to the dais where his family sat. His parents held the center seats, with Joseph's place at his father's left empty and waiting for him and his youngest sibling, Pyter, in the next seat. Neane's place to their mother's right was also empty, but Eve and Rebecca chatted from their seats.

Gibril's chair stood empty. The only one of Uncle Michael's brood to attend this year was probably off tending to her own amusements. Knowing Gibby, those amusements consisted of teasing young lords with her approaching adulthood and budding availability. Joseph was glad none of his sisters enjoyed that game. Keen men were a fiercely sexual lot, almost equal to the females they pursued.

He brushed away several unwelcome advances on his way to his father's side. Life was no easier for Joseph than it was for Neane. Though Uncle Michael was next in line for the throne if Jole died before Michael did, Michael had abdicated that role long ago, and Joseph was heir apparent. Few noblewomen weren't on the hunt to become the next queen.

He flicked glances at Neane as he crossed the ballroom. She moved steadily, her head tipped down, seemingly not finding what she sought. Joseph ached for her. He couldn't imagine what it would be like to find someone to share your life with only to lose the chance to follow that path.

"Why so tense, Joseph?" his father asked as he sank into his chair.

Joseph leaned back in the padded throne, crossing his legs at the ankle and steepling his hands in front of his face. "Escaping my avid admirers, Father."

"When the right one appears, you'll know it."

"Hmm." Joseph knew it, but he had to bide his time. He watched Neane out of the corner of his eye. He just hoped Neane knew it as fully as he did.

She stilled, meeting a man's eyes, then turned and made her way out of the ballroom. Joseph's heart beat hard against his ribs.

He reasoned himself calmer. Neane was inside the palace. One scream would bring the guards.

The man glanced toward the dais, smiling widely. He turned and followed Neane.

Joseph swallowed a sour wave. Lord Byen was the man Neane sought? *Please Fion! Let her see what poison that man is.* Byen wasn't meant for her. Joseph wouldn't wish that undisciplined buck wariken on Gibby.

"Joseph?" their mother called. "Where is your twin sister?"

Byen disappeared from view.

For a fleeting moment, Joseph considered sending Panor after her—or going himself, but he'd given his word that he'd leave her in peace. "I don't know, Mother." *Fion, protect her. Neane isn't ready for a man like Byen.*

CHAPTER TWO

Tirin turned, trying to fix the direction of the woman's voice.

"I said 'take your hands off of me'," she ordered.

"Why did you invite me to come here with you if you didn't want me?" the man asked in amusement.

"I didn't ask you, Byen. You're drunk. Now unhand me."

Tirin started toward the voices, fisting his hand in fury as the woman let out a squeak of protest. Byen was known as a rake, but even *he* didn't typically stoop to forcing his attentions on women.

"Ow," Byen complained. "That was uncalled for."

Tirin swerved right around a line of hedges. They were close.

"I gave you fair warning," the woman barked. "Now release me, before I do worse."

"Be still and talk to me," he growled. "Ow! That's it."

Her cry of alarm was muffled. As Tirin rounded the statue of Fion, he saw the reason why.

Byen held her tight to his body with an arm up the middle of her back, one of her arms immobilized against his body and the other trapped at above the elbow in his grip. He had her bent back over the plane of the restraining arm, attempting to force his kiss on her. The woman's neck was extended past any illusion of comfort, Byen's hand fisted in her hair, holding her still for his assault.

She beat at him, but her position left the woman little room for attack. Her fingernails rasped against the collar of Byen's jacket, seeking to scratch sense into him.

Byen pressed her to the trunk of an Eir tree, releasing her hair once he'd forced her body to his to do the job. The rogue stroked her breast with his free hand, his fingers tracing the silin bodice to the upper edge, then curling inside while she tried to twist away from him.

Tirin grabbed Byen by the back of his hair and yanked him off the struggling woman. He cringed at the sound of ripping silin and her soft cry of alarm.

She swung out of his grip on the pivot point of Byen's hand on her arm, a dizzying movement, even to someone watching it. She punched Byen hard across the cheek with a sound halfway between a grunt and a cry of frustration, then grasped at the torn shoulder of her dress. Her hair tumbled down over her shoulders from the hair clip Byen had all but ripped from her tresses.

Byen released her and turned toward Tirin, reaching for his dagger. Tirin moved faster. His punch carried much more force than the woman's had. Byen collapsed to the ground, and Tirin let him fall.

He reached for the woman automatically, trying to gauge her injuries with a muttered prayer that any she'd suffered were minor. The psychological effects of the attack would be damaging enough. She recoiled, slipping away from his touch and pulling her fist back to strike again, trembling hard.

Tirin put his hands up in a calming gesture. "I won't hurt you. You have my vow as an officer on that. Are you hurt?"

She shook her head. "Thank you," she managed in a shaky voice, motioning to Byen. "Thank you for that, Captain Tirin."

She pulled at the clip in her hair, her hand quaking so hard she nearly dropped it. Forsaking appearances, the woman released the dress and let it dip, uncovering the upper swell of her breast as she swept her hair back and used the clip to hold it off her face.

He stilled, trying to identify her in the pale moonlight that escaped the clouds. The jeweled choker caught his eyes first. Who had he seen in such a choker? Tirin cupped her chin up to catch the moonlight on her face. She gasped. Wide eyes stared up at him, pale eyes that were most probably green.

Tirin pulled his hand back as if she burned him, dropping his gaze respectfully. Princess Jenneane wasn't his to touch. "Forgive me, Princess. If you'll come with me, I'll arrange for Byen—"

"No," she ordered quickly. "Thank you, but I'll be going now."

"Going? Byen—"

"Is drunk," she interrupted him.

"It's no excuse." *Damn it! I'm looking at her face again. Oh well, I am talking to her.*

"It's no reason to kill him, either." She turned away and headed for a half-hidden door in the palace wall.

Tirin stalked after her. "He attacked you," he thundered.

Jenneane motioned to him for silence. "Are you insane?" she whispered. "Do you have any concept what will happen if I am found like this?"

He dropped his voice to a growl that matched his level of frustration. "Yes. Your father will kill Byen, as he deserves."

"And place me under heavy guard. Any man who dares look at me will suffer for Byen's stupidity."

A streak of pure fury lit in Tirin's mind. "Your flirting would suffer a catastrophic setback," he accused.

Her mouth moved as if to protest, but only a gasping breath emerged. Jenneane stiffened her spine. "I have a duty to fulfill. I'm sure you're well aware of it, considering your bid for my attention." She turned away and slipped through the door and down a flight of stairs into a musty smelling room, Tirin at her heels.

"A duty?" he asked in disbelief.

"Yes. A duty. What? You think there's a love match in store for me?" She laughed harshly, then uttered something in her mother's language. "The best I can hope for is to marry a man I won't despise in a decade."

"What was that?"

Jenneane looked at him in confusion.

"What you said in English?"

"I called you a rather rude Earth name. It

wasn't very complimentary, and I do owe you a debt of thanks, so I did it in English to avoid offending you."

Tirin forced his jaw to unlock. "Back to this duty."

She sighed and headed across the room, finding her way in the shaft of moonlight that came through the pane of glass in the heavy door. "Yes, Captain?"

"There are better ways to fulfill it than making yourself..."

"Say it. You've made yourself clear. You think I enjoy the attention."

"Don't you?" The rumors about the palace were that Princess Jenneane enjoyed the attention quite a bit...with most any lord who wanted to play with the pretty princess. Tirin scowled. When had he started believing palace rumors?

"No. I don't. Not that you would believe me, but it's true."

"Then why do you allow it?"

"It's that or watch a whole string of overzealous, stupid, desperate men cut down trying to get close to me. So, I allow them to get close until I can't stand it anymore. Then I take my leave."

Tirin winced. Her logic made a certain amount of sense. "Did you ever find a man you wanted to let close?"

She hesitated. "Once."

Only once? Perhaps the rumors were wrong. She certainly sounded sincere. "What happened?"

"He—wasn't interested, I suppose."

"What? Why?" *And, who could be such a*

monumental fool?

"I'm still trying to figure that out."

A rustle of fabric caught his attention. "What are you doing?" Tirin could see the vague outlines of Jenneane's body in the near-darkness but not enough to tell what she was up to.

"Removing this torn gown."

Tirin hardened. He gripped her upper arms, ignoring the nagging voice in his mind telling him that he shouldn't touch her. If Tirin didn't stop her, he'd do something stupid. "Don't," he growled.

* * * *

Jenneane closed her eyes, feeling the tense muscles of Tirin's chest through the two layers of silin as if she were nude. She licked her lip and fought to control her breathing. "You shouldn't," she whispered. "You shouldn't touch me."

You really shouldn't. Fion! He feels so good. She resisted the urge to press her back further into him.

"Don't take that dress off," he ordered.

"Why?" Her voice squeaked a bit. Jenneane shook herself mentally. Tirin was just a man. Men threw themselves at her on a regular basis.

Tirin pulled her back into his body. Jenneane swallowed a moan of pleasure as she felt his erect cock press to the small of her back.

"You're no innocent, Princess. I'm sure you recognize a fiercely aroused male. I have more self-control than Byen does, but even I can't be pushed that far. The dress stays."

His words tumbled in her mind. Tirin wanted her. He was at the edges of control with her. Her stomach quivered in a strange awareness at the realization. Jenneane wanted him to lose control. The idea of Tirin out of control was strangely arousing.

A niggling of unease sent waves through the already choppy waters of her mind. "No innocent?" she croaked. "Recognize a— What are you accusing me of, Captain?"

His breath was hot on her shoulder, sending tendrils of that heat snaking through her body. He was close enough to kiss.

"I've seen them in the palace corridors today," he spat.

"Seen who?"

"The schaen. I know they're not your mother's, and your sisters are too young to have a schaen group yet, as memory serves."

Jenneane elbowed him in the ribs, pushing Tirin away from her as he grunted, shivering as his hands left her body. The realization that she felt loss made her angrier still. "They happen to be Gibril's schaen. I don't believe in the practice, Captain. Don't ever compare me to my cousin."

"I—I apologize," he stammered.

"As well you should. Go away, Captain. You are dismissed. I don't need your protection or your help in finding my rooms."

"It is my duty to protect you."

So, I'm a duty? That thought hurt. Couldn't he *want* to protect her?

Jenneane moved to the foot of the ladder and went back to work on her dress without answering. *Captain Tirin's libido be damned!* She couldn't climb in the ball gown.

"Please don't do this," he begged.

"I'm not nude, Captain. I'm still wearing my costume beneath the dress."

He groaned as if he were in pain. "I'm not sure that is much of an improvement."

"You'll live."

* * * *

Joseph tensed as Panor stormed toward the dais. He had hoped Neane was back in her rooms, but the look on the security chief's face promised death to someone, and there were few things that would push Panor so far.

Panor leaned between Joseph and his father. "I must speak with you, Majesty."

Jole sighed. "Tell me."

"A guest has been attacked."

"What?" Jole and Joseph demanded in unison.

Joseph's vague sense of unease gelled into a certainty that there was a reason he'd not seen Neane again. "Who and where, Panor?" he asked urgently.

The other two men cast intent stares his way.

Joseph shifted nervously. "Who and where?" he replied slowly, as calmly as he could manage.

"In the garden, Highness. It was Lord Byen. Unfortunately, he is unconscious. The only evidence we have is this scrap of—"

Joseph snatched the green silin in shaking fingers, an image of the dress Neane wore dancing in his mind and searing in his gut like a torch. "Call out your men."

"Highness?"

"Now, Panor. I want every available— Why didn't I go after her?" he breathed.

His father's eyes widened. Jole panned his gaze over his assembled children. "Who?" he asked weakly, noting as Joseph did that he was two daughters short.

Joseph handed the scrap back to Panor. "Neane. She... I knew Byen left the room after her, but I thought she was safely inside the palace."

Panor shook his head. "You're mistaken. The princess was in black, and my men followed her to her rooms when she left the ballroom."

"The first time she left," Joseph insisted. "She changed clothes and came back down."

"My men would have seen—"

Joseph glared at him, and Panor fell silent.

"Why?" Jole demanded. "Why did she sneak off?"

He cleared his throat. "She wanted to meet a man, a man she likes."

"Who?"

"She wouldn't tell me," Joseph admitted.

"And you let her go?" his father thundered.

"Here to the ballroom...with fifty armed guards," he replied weakly.

Panor nodded. "Could Byen be the man she was meeting?"

Joseph shrugged. "I hope not. I always thought Neane had better taste than that."

Chapter Three

Tirin ground his teeth as his hand brushed the silin covering Jenneane's ankle. He cursed the darkness in the ladder well that caused him to touch her even as he thanked Fion for Her mercy in sending that darkness.

Were it not for that small favor, Tirin would be far too tempted to fix his undivided attention on the silin-encased body above him. He was painfully erect at the thought of the outline of the cleft in her bottom as she climbed, the snug fit of the garment over her breasts, thighs, and the core of her being nestled between those thighs.

Tirin shivered as his hand encountered the silin again. He'd had ample view of that outfit in the dim light before they made it deep into the well. Would that he had hours to explore that body—and the right to do it.

"How far does this reach?" he asked quietly.

"It reaches to the second floor, but we'll be getting off at the first."

Good. We're almost there. Even with the high ceilings in the palace, their climb had to be nearly ended.

Jenneane stepped onto a ledge, and a shower of pebbles and grit cascaded over him.

"Sorry," she muttered. "Are you all right down there?"

Tirin shook his hair and rubbed the dirt from his cheeks. "Yes. Coming up. Move back if you can." He straightened his jacket as he stood, grimacing at what he must look like. His hair was mussed. He was filthy, and his uniform jacket and tunic were likely ruined. Even his boots were scuffed—perhaps beyond repair.

"Follow the ledge carefully in my direction," Jenneane instructed.

"Why are we doing this?"

"You know another way to get to my rooms without being seen?"

"I didn't know *this* one," he grumbled. *I wish I didn't now.*

"Well now you do. This is the most difficult part. It's a simple task after this."

"That would be refreshing," Tirin noted sarcastically.

"I didn't ask you to accompany me."

"I had to have some excuse for not turning Byen over to Panor and your father. If I'm keeping you out of trouble, I have a greater purpose and ample reason for dereliction in that duty."

"I don't need you to keep me out of trouble," Jenneane snapped.

"I noticed that."

"If you're finished, Captain, I can get us out of here, so you can return to your normal duties."

Tirin fisted his hand in frustration. Did the woman acknowledge that she needed anyone? And why would Tirin care if she needed him?

Jenneane twisted on the ledge and pulled a wooden bar up. Tirin held his breath as decades-old metal hinges creaked. Soft light filtered from the small door she opened. She set the bar down carefully and grasped the rock face, planting the toe of her right boot in the cracks between the stones.

Tirin sighed. Jenneane was the most stubborn woman he'd ever met. He clasped her waist in his hands, intent on lifting her to the opening. She flailed, twisting in his arms. He tightened his grip with a curse, forcing Jenneane into the wall behind her as her balance shifted toward the drop. The wooden bar clattered to the floor below. She shook in his arms, wincing as the bar splintered. They stared at each other, their breathing coming in sharp tandem gasps.

"What in Len's Underworld are you doing?" he demanded in a hoarse whisper.

"How dare you touch me." Her protest was weak, without the conviction he'd expected would accompany it. She prodded at his chest, a gentle reminder to release her.

He pretended not to notice. Jenneane was still shaking, and Tirin wasn't about to chance her safety, just because she was being obstinate. "You pick the oddest times to balk at a man's touch," he commented coolly.

"What do you think you're doing?"

"I was helping you through the opening."

"I don't need your help," she informed him with a tilt of her chin in challenge. "I've been doing this without help since I was ten. I happen to be an expert climber, Captain."

"You don't wish my help?" he growled.

"I don't."

Tirin nodded curtly and released her.

Jenneane took a shuddering breath. She turned to the wall and climbed to the opening like an expert rock smith, though she shook so badly that Tirin braced himself to catch her if she fell. She swung her legs up and lifted her upper body with arms of a trained athlete.

When she disappeared through the tiny doorway, he started up after her. Two slipped footholds, five curses, and a ripped trouser knee later, Tirin emerged behind her, sweating and panting. He looked around at the laundry room curiously.

"How did you do that?" he asked.

"My Uncle Michael suggested that all of us should be trained in survival skills in the Garesh Mountains—in all seasons."

Tirin grimaced. "Survival training?" The Garesh Mountains were Len's Dungeons in the winter. Why would he suggest something so—Tirin bit off the thought that Michael had always been called 'the mad re-bred.'

A smile pulled at her lips. "Ever eaten redgrass roots and cracker tack?"

"Unfortunately. Yes. In training."

"A little Eir sap, and it's not entirely horrible."

Tirin chuckled lightly. "I'll try to remember that."

She glanced back at him and made a pained face. Jenneane snatched up a cleansing cloth and wet it in the deep sink.

Tirin closed his eyes as she started cleaning the dirt from his face. "What are you—"

"Shhh. I'll replace your uniform. This is my fault."

"Not necessary," he managed. Tirin fisted his hands behind his back, willing himself not to touch her. He opened his eyes as the cloth moved to his neck...then wished he hadn't.

Jenneane stared at the path the cloth took, biting her lip lightly. Her breathing was quick, and her breasts jumped with every sharp intake of air. Tirin's body responded, his cock pressing against the buttons on his trousers.

She continued, oblivious to his state. Jenneane pulled the last two ties on his tunic open, and the cloth caressed more of his body, matting the dark curls she'd uncovered to his chest.

Tirin hissed out a breath as the cloth found one male nipple. She stilled, snapping a look at his face...a look that implied she had forgotten he stood looking down at her. Jenneane looked at his cock and offered an explicative in English.

"Another less-than-complimentary comment about my person?" he joked, trying to regain his self-control.

Jenneane swallowed hard. "Uh. No. Not uncomplimentary at all."

Tirin shuddered. *That attitude certainly isn't helping.* "I think you should stop now, Jenneane."

She nodded and pulled her hand away. Jenneane turned abruptly, rinsing the cloth and scrubbing at her face and neck.

That isn't helping, either. Is she trying to drive me mad? Tirin bit back a groan as she slid the cloth beneath the edge of her silin costume. "What do we do now?" *Why did I ask that? If she says something sexual, I am lost.*

"Well, we could have gone up to the second floor in the ladder well and come out in the war room, but since we're this far, we can't go back that way."

"Was that exit harder to get out of?" he asked in surprise. What antics did Jenneane engage in? If it was even as hard as the lower one, at that height, the fall—

"No. Easier." She tossed the cloth into the sink.

"Heavily guarded?"

"Under normal circumstances, it's less guarded than what we're about to do."

Tirin shook his head. "Then why are we going this way?"

"Two reasons. On the remote chance that someone is watching for me, that is the route they will expect me to take."

"And the other reason?" he prodded.

"I'm starving. I can never eat at these ridiculous celebrations."

* * * *

"I don't understand it," Panor complained. "None of the guards recall a woman coming in from the gardens dressed in a green silin gown. Peahl remembers her going out, just as you describe, with Byen only moments behind."

Joseph shook his head. "She came back. I know she did." He tapped his finger on the window glass. "Where in the gardens?"

"Where?" Jole echoed.

Joseph grimaced. "We had entrances we used as children. If she could reach one without passing a guard, Neane would use it." He turned and met Panor's startled look. "Where in the gardens?"

The security chief shook his head. "Near the stand of Eir trees. Outside the meditation circle."

"Near the statue of Fion?" Joseph asked excitedly.

"Four body-length from the statue, Highness."

"Yes!" He bolted for the door with Panor and his father at his heels.

"Where are you going?" Jole shouted as Joseph brushed past a guard scrambling to attention for them.

"Where she did." Joseph sprinted around the palace wall, dodging guards, making a straight line for the ancient storehouse.

"Where?" Jole thundered.

Joseph dragged the door open and grinned at his father.

"There's no way out," Panor argued.

"Of course there is," Joseph assured him. He dropped down the stairs and went to the ladder well, scooping up the dress. "She's been here."

Panor took it, passing a small pocket light over it carefully. "Byen tore the shoulder. That is the silin in his hand. But, if the dress is here—" He snapped a look at Jole, then lowered his gaze slowly.

Jole nodded stiffly. "Where does this come out?" he demanded.

Joseph sighed. "Two exits. First floor comes out in the service area—laundry. Jenneane will come out on the second floor."

"Why?" Panor asked.

"It opens on the opposite side of the war room

from the King's corridors. It's a straight line from here to her room...without passing any guards."

CHAPTER FOUR

"Mmm. This is good." Tirin took another bite of the pastry as they lounged in a darkened hallway near the bakery kitchen.

Jenneane had lamented that they couldn't chance the main kitchen, but he noticed she ate a fair share of the pastries she'd stolen for them. The princess was quite the accomplished little thief.

"Joseph and I figured out a way to get to the kitchens at every manor and palace first thing. Father and Mother always had the finest cooks."

"Of course." Tirin licked a dab of icing off of his lips. "Do you like Gelgrin?"

Jenneane grinned. "I love it."

"Our cook makes a Gelgrin that melts in your mouth. I understand that Kell Ri tried to steal his predecessor from my parents' employ for his personal recipe. His son is our current cook. I'll send you some."

"I'd like that." She peeked into the hall. "Come on. The way will be clear for at least a quarter hour now."

Tirin stuffed the last of the pastry into his mouth and followed Jenneane down the corridor. He watched in shock as she pushed open a hidden panel in the carved Eir wood wall and waved him into the passageway beyond it.

Jenneane closed the door behind him. "Watch your feet. Portions of the walls have crumbled away."

"Is this safe?"

"Perfectly. Trust me." Jenneane turned up the stone steps without hesitation.

Tirin followed her. "You use these often?"

"No. I used to when I was a child. Not often now."

"How did you escape your guards?"

Jenneane shot him a look of disbelief. "You're in centuries-old hidden corridors that only palace residents, ancient historians, and architectural enthusiasts know exist and only a half dozen people outside the royal family know the entrances to, and you want to know how I did it? Unbelievable."

"Why does no one know about them?"

"Every palace has had these same corridors. By tradition, all the palaces have been based on Ro Ti's designs. The uses for some of the rooms change, but the royal chambers, ballroom, war room, kitchens, offices, and these corridors stay the same. It's—symbolic, I guess, of the dark years of upheaval."

"That makes about as much sense as any of our traditions," Tirin asserted. *No. Some of them make sense. Jenneane wouldn't have been attacked, if those traditions had been upheld.*

"That was my thought," she agreed.

Tirin locked on the sway of her hips, on the curve and cleft of her buttocks outlined perfectly in the second skin of her costume. "Why?" he breathed.

"Why what?"

"Why did you duck your guards? Why did you change clothes?"

Jenneane tripped. Tirin captured her waist, setting her back on her feet. His fingers lingered a moment, and she took a calming breath. Tirin forced his hands down again. She resumed climbing the stone stairs, shaking lightly.

"Why?" he asked again.

"I was looking for someone, trying to find him in the crowd."

"Byen?" he spat.

She turned abruptly, and Tirin came face to glorious cleavage with her. It was a long, agonizing moment before he reminded himself to move back from her body. His heart pounded in his chest.

"Sorry," he grumbled. "Watching my feet."

"You think I'm stupid enough to have anything to do with Byen?" Jenneane demanded in a fierce whisper.

Tirin shook his head. "Not really."

"Good." She turned on her heel in a precision move and crossed her arms over her chest, taking the stairs more forcefully.

"Who was he?"

"Why? Planning on telling my father?"

"No. I just want to know."

"Why?"

Yes, Tirin. Why would you care?

"I don't know," he snapped. "I just do."

"Well, it doesn't matter, does it? It *flopped*."

"Flopped?" *Damn Jenneane and her English euphemisms.*

"Failed. It didn't work out."

"How does a tryst with a woman like you go wrong?"

"You are going to compare me to my cousin

once too often, Captain. It was not a tryst. It was me trying to find the man so I could meet him without a crowd of admirers prodding at me. I am not in the habit of having *trysts.*"

Tirin smiled. "Have you noticed that every time you get angry with me, you call me Captain?"

"Eedeot mael fowk," she breathed.

"Is that the same thing you called me last time?" he asked lightly.

"Effectively," she replied shortly. "Jagouf."

"Oh, a new one," Tirin noted, secretly cheering the fact that he could antagonize Jenneane as easily as she could antagonize him.

"My insults aren't improving."

"Good. Who was he?" *And why do I care?*

* * * *

Jenneane sighed. Did this man ever shut up? Tirin was the most infuriating, pigheaded male she'd ever met. Considering she'd met her father, her twin brother, Panor, and 'Pappy' Pyter, it was saying a lot that Tirin was worse than all of them.

"Jenneane? Who was he?" His voice was quickly becoming an order.

"That's none of your concern, is it?"

"It is," he insisted.

"I don't see how."

Tirin punched the stone wall. Jenneane looked at him curiously. His muscles were bunched under his jacket, and his jaw was set, a muscle twitching below his ear.

Jenneane turned and hurried along, her body

rioting. Tirin appeared... Was there a term for it? Possessive? Protective?

She stilled as she heard sounds echoing down the stone corridor.

"What is—" Tirin began.

She turned and clapped a hand over his mouth, forcing her breathing to shallow as she listened for the sound to repeat. "Oh no," Jenneane whispered. "Quiet. Come with me."

Tirin nodded and let her lead him by a hand on his wrist. Jenneane slid into the checkpoint, a room the size of a large clothes cabinet with a narrow door and no windows to the corridor.

"What is—" Tirin began again.

"Shhh. In here."

He scowled but he squeezed in and closed the door. The moon was hidden behind the clouds, and the room was nearly pitch black with the door pulled shut.

"Is there a light?" he breathed next to her ear.

"It would be seen in the corridor."

Tirin shifted against her, closer than he needed to be. "Why are we hiding?"

"The guards are in the corridors. They'll do a sweep and move on."

He nodded, the slight stubble on his cheek brushing her face. Jenneane turned her head, savoring the feel of him against her lips.

"Don't," Tirin warned her.

Jenneane ran her hands over his chest, finding his male nipples already hardened. "Why?"

His breathing hitched. Tirin's hands closed on her hips, and he drew her to his body. The ridge of his cock pressed to her stomach. Jenneane panted through clenched teeth, her womb hot and heavy, moisture soaking the silin between her thighs.

"I will respond, Jenneane."

"Have you noticed that you call me Jenneane?" Her heels left the floor and she pressed her lips to his, opening to invite him in.

Tirin ran his hands up her silin-clad body until he caressed her bare shoulders. His kiss was slow and thorough, exploring every corner of her mouth, moving deep inside her until Jenneane was dizzy in desire.

He started to pull back as the footsteps closed on their position, but she rose further on tiptoe to encourage him. Tirin eased her to the wall, rocking his hips in mute demonstration—or appeal. Jenneane grasped his shoulders, hoisting herself as she had in the ladder well. She wrapped her legs over his hips, seating Tirin's erect length to her aching core and finding only a greater need for her trouble.

"Well, I can assure Panor that there's no one in that section of the corridors," a soldier commented.

Tirin stilled, his mouth leaving hers. He buried his face in her throat, tracing the edge of the choker with his tongue. Jenneane fought to keep her breathing slow and even, to focus on anything outside of how Tirin was destroying her concentration with his mouth and body.

He picked that moment to stroke one of her puckered nipples. Jenneane ground her teeth at the waves of pleasure that started at his fingertips and crested deep in her womb. She dug her fingernails into the rough weave of his uniform jacket.

"Find anything, Lieutenant?" a new voice asked.

Tirin found a new form of torture for her. Were it not for the punishment if he were caught this way, Jenneane would have sworn he wanted to drive her into revealing herself to the guards. He lifted her away from his cock; his mouth closed on a breast, and his tongue flicked over the rigid nipple, setting up a pulse for him that radiated through her thighs and womb.

"No. I didn't expect that we would, but Panor was adamant."

"We'd better check in. You know how he is when he's anxious."

The lieutenant groaned. "Unfortunately, the whole palace knows."

Tirin switched breasts, moving his hips in time to his ministrations, sliding the silin bodysuit against her inner thighs, enflaming her further. Jenneane fisted her hands in his hair, holding him to her while she bit her lip in restraint. It seemed to take forever for the guards' footsteps to fade away. Her body burned for him. Her nerves tingled and pulsed, making her entire body ache in need. Jenneane pushed his jacket back, pulling up at his tunic.

He grasped her hands, letting her settle against his cock again. "No," Tirin breathed, raising his face to hers.

"Tirin, I need—" Jenneane knew very well what she needed. Syl and her mother had trained her in her solemn duty since she was a child, but Jenneane had never realized the urge to mate could be so strong. She shivered in anticipation.

"Not like this."

"I thought it was going well," she quipped, hiding the hurt of his refusal as best she could.

"You're intact, aren't you?" Tirin asked gravely. "I know Joseph has taken schente, but you don't believe in schaen or empty trysts. I know you don't."

Jenneane nodded, feeling her face heat, knowing Tirin could see her blush in the moonlight now streaming through the narrow window.

Tirin touched her face gently. "I won't do this."

"But—" *Tirin didn't balk at getting me in this state of arousal, but he won't give me relief.*

"I will not take your maiden's barrier against a dirty stone wall. I won't take it at all until..."

Her breathing hitched. "Until when?"

"Who was he? The man you went back to meet? Who did you want to find in the crowd?"

Jenneane pressed a kiss to his jaw. "I found him."

"What are you saying?"

"I was looking for you." She met his eyes in the faint light filtering through the window.

"For... Why?"

"Do you realize what an unusual man you are?"

Tirin shook his head, his eyes wide.

"You wanted me. Your eyes told me that, but you didn't touch me. You barely spoke to me or looked at me. You showed me respect. You didn't press your case like the others."

"What did you want from me?"

"I...don't know." Jenneane eased her legs down, suddenly nervous about being held in Tirin's arms. "I needed to know if you saw me."

Tirin didn't release her. "How could I not see you?"

"Do you know how many lords have ever asked if I liked Gelgrin? Or where I learned to climb? I'd wager none of them know those things. They don't want to know them. You did. You are the first man who—" She shook her head.

"No one has ever bothered to find out who you are?"

"No. So you see, you were so very different, I had to know."

He took a calming breath. "Know?" he whispered.

"If there was something more."

* * * *

Tirin pulled her to his chest. He fought for a decent breath. All this time, Jenneane had wanted him, and Tirin had all but called her a wanton during their flight. Had he gotten to know her before he came to his own conclusions about her?

He cleared his throat. "A contract?"

Tirin wanted that. The realization had come somewhere between Jenneane cleaning his face and that first kiss, but he'd wanted her for more than sex earlier—possibly when he'd learned that she hated her life but saw no better prospects. He could offer more. Tirin would give anything to show Jenneane that there was more to a contract than she expected.

Jenneane pulled at a curl over her ear, twisting it around her fingers. She didn't meet his eyes. "Would you really offer that?" she asked nervously.

Tirin smiled, cupping her chin and raising her face. "I'll offer tonight, if you're willing."

She nodded, looking stunned. A mischievous smile curved her lips, and he could see her face darken all the way down to that enticing choker in the dim light. "Was the contract the 'until'?" she asked in a conspiratorial tone.

He nodded, fighting back the urge to make a liar of himself. There were forms, appearances, safeguards... There were too many reasons not to finish here.

Jenneane slid by his body and pushed the door open. She peeked down the corridors and waved Tirin after her. He watched the sway of her hips, grinding his teeth as he hardened further. Tirin gave up any pretense of following the laws. He wanted her, and as soon as the contract was sealed, he would do a lot more than look at Jenneane.

Mag help any other man who doesn't live the mores to the letter once the contract is sealed. Any man who dared look at Jenneane or touch her then would face Tirin at his worst. He opened his mouth to ask her to have her father enforce the mores now, but Jenneane motioned him for quiet.

She eased open a peek hole and surveyed the room beyond. Jenneane pushed open a narrow door with a sigh and stepped into a dimly-lit but very lavish bedroom.

A huge four poster bed was hung with heavy, dark drapes in the royal red, closed for the night save a slight break, the gold cord ties arranged in ornate bows by diligent servants. There was thick white carpet on the floor that spoke of daily cleansing and shelves of bound books on the walls. A full-length Eir-framed mirror reflected his image from the far wall.

Tirin hesitated, reluctant to place himself in danger of being found in what was undoubtedly Jenneane's bedroom.

She shot him a look of confusion. "Well, come on," she invited.

Tirin ducked into the room, fighting back a near panic. "This is a terrible idea. If the guards come in here—"

Jenneane laughed. "Why would they? As far as anyone knows, I've been in this room for hours."

"Maybe. If no one discovered Byen unconscious, and he made it off the grounds without being seen."

"And how would that be connected to me?" she asked in that same conspiratorial tone she'd used in the checkpoint.

"Well, he—" Tirin chuckled. "You're right. Byen can't admit how he ended up that way without losing his head for it."

Her smile widened. "Exactly."

He shifted toward her then halted, restraining the urge to nestle to her warm body and whisper directly into her ear. "You know, I should take personal offense to how easily you evade royal guards, Jenneane," he chided playfully.

"But since it comes in so handy..." Jenneane sauntered toward him, her body in a sensual dance. "It occurs to me that I still haven't thanked you for dealing with Byen for me." She laid a hand on his stomach...then the other.

His breathing went strangled. "You thanked me."

Jenneane ran her fingertips up Tirin's chest and knit them behind his neck. "Not properly," she whispered.

Tirin's cock ached. It would be a long night of self-release in punishment for letting her touch him again, but he couldn't deny his need to touch her. "What is a proper thank you for knocking a—"

He got no further. Their kiss was unrestrained. There was no gentle exploration involved in this kiss. Jenneane set out to seduce him, and he set out to conquer her. Tirin cupped her buttocks and pulled her to his aching body, reminding himself that he couldn't follow through yet. He pulled away in resignation.

Jenneane smiled. "That gets better every time we do it," she sighed.

Tirin nodded. "I need to go."

"Now?" she asked in disbelief.

"Now. Immediately." *Before I break every law there is on this matter.*

Her smile disappeared. That heartbreaking look of hurt was back on her face. "Why now?"

"I have to find your father and offer that contract..." He ran a hand over his jacket, grimacing. "Uh... Maybe I should clean up first, but then I need to find him—quickly. I may go insane if I don't."

"You've offered it, and I've accepted it. My father is just a formality."

"A formality who will gladly take my head for this," Tirin argued.

"For what?"

"I think what we've been doing would definitely qualify as me laying hands on you."

Jenneane scowled. "It's not as if *that* has been punishable so far," she noted sarcastically.

"That stops now, Jenneane," he ordered. "For once, that pack of wariken will mind their borders. They won't look at you, and the next one who dares touch you will taste my blade, if your father doesn't get there first."

"I won't argue that point." She sounded weary.

"You'd better not," Tirin growled. "I know you hate it."

"Laying hands not being a crime yet, there is no reason for you to leave tonight."

"The contract," he reminded her with an arched eyebrow.

"My parents didn't wait for one," she pleaded.

"That's different. Your mother was—"

"Born a Keen princess, just as I was."

"Born on Earth," he continued. "Which means she and your father had a different set of rules. The law assumed she belonged to him. The law assumes I could be killed for that kiss you just gave me."

"My father didn't think it made any difference if Mother was born on Earth or Kegin, Tirin. If it made no difference to them—"

Tirin bit back a smile. "You are tempting me," he warned her.

"Good. You're the one who got me in this state. You deserve to suffer with me—or to find relief with me," Jenneane offered with a sly grin.

He pulled her hand to the throbbing head of his cock, shooting her a hard look as he pressed her hand flat under his to it. "Oh, I am suffering, Jenneane."

She pulled her hand from under his, tracing the ridge slowly. "You don't have to."

Tirin groaned. "What in Len's Underworld am I going to do with you?"

"I've already told you that."

"But, we should—"

Her fingers plucked at the buttons on his trousers, not quite undoing them but making Tirin aware of how far she would go to convince him. His protest died in his throat, and the reasons behind it seemed to scatter on the wind.

Jenneane pressed her body to his, no doubt well aware of how she affected him. "We have a bed this time. We're not in a filthy corridor. You did say—"

He kissed her, guiding Jenneane back to the curtained bed. His hands worked the tiny hooks on the back of her costume, ripping a few off entirely in his haste. "I'll find your father in the morning," he breathed, tasting her mouth again.

There are reasons, his rational mind protested. But what those reasons were, he couldn't place while she was in his arms and aroused.

"As if your mother doesn't have a contract prepared," she teased.

"Not one I want you to sign," he admitted. "Tell

me what you want, Jenneane."

Tirin had to say the ritual words now. There would be no stopping once he had this damned costume off of her. Nothing else mattered to him. Not securing a contract. Not the fact that guards were searching the corridors behind the walls. Not even the tradition of having a woman healer present for her first mating. This was their moment, and that moment would be now.

"Hello, Jenneane." The bedside lamp switched on, and the drapes slid back with an ominous hiss of metal on metal not unlike the test of a blade.

Tirin stilled, his face buried in her hair, three-quarters of the line of hooks to her waist unclasped, and his rock-hard cock pressed to her stomach. He raised his head slowly, swallowing a growl of frustration...or perhaps a lump of fear.

Jenneane dropped her forehead to his bare chest, between the unbuttoned uniform jacket and untied tunic. "Fowk," she grumbled.

He took a calming breath, nodding his agreement. Tirin had no idea what the Earth sentiment meant, but with Jole Ri sitting on his daughter's bed, listening to every word they'd said since entering the room, Tirin could guess how harsh a curse it was.

CHAPTER FIVE

She didn't move for a long moment. His oldest daughter stood with her nearly-bare back to Jole, her face pressed to the Captain's equally-unclothed chest.

"Jenneane," Jole growled in warning. The least he deserved was her attention, all things considered.

She turned to face him, crossing her arms over her chest as the costume slipped, placing herself between the tousled guard captain and her father. Jole almost laughed at that. Jenneane had always had spirit, but that move was a bit beyond anything he'd ever expected of her. Of course, this entire night fit into that category.

"Where have you been?" Jole asked, forcing an even tone.

There were too many questions that needed to be answered before he decided what to do about this situation. After more than an hour of heart-stopping fear for her, finding Jenneane in a cozy little romp with a guard captain was the last thing Jole wanted to see.

He pushed away thoughts of the less-welcome alternatives. Okay, there *were* worse things he could have seen.

Jenneane swallowed what looked like a painful lump. "Making our way back here—tunnels, back passageways, and the King's corridors."

Jole surveyed the captain's torn clothing and

abraded knuckles, Jenneane's knotted hair, their dirt-streaked faces and scuffed boots, pausing momentarily at her reddened knuckles. "Are you injured?"

She shook her head.

The captain—*Tirin, she called him*—put a hand on her shoulder in comfort.

Jole bristled at that, but he may still owe this man a vow of thanks. It was too early to decide. "What did Byen do, Captain Tirin?"

The young man took a deep breath. "He—tried to take liberties Her Highness didn't offer, Majesty."

"Aren't you being a bit too formal, Captain Tirin? She was 'Jenneane' only moments ago...while you were busy stripping off her clothing."

Tirin shot a pained look at Jenneane, moving his hand to his side reluctantly as he darkened. "That could be taken as a warning or a comment, Majesty. I know not your mind."

"When I'm sure, I'll let you know," Jole growled, only marginally mollified that Tirin wasn't touching her anymore.

Jenneane grimaced. "That was a warning," she muttered.

Tirin nodded. "I know."

Jole rubbed his forehead. "What liberties?" he asked.

Byen would have to be dealt with harshly. Depending on the facts, Jole might be forced to make the ultimate example of the young lord.

"He was drunk," Jenneane dismissed the question.

"Immaterial," Jole barked.

Tirin bit back a smile rather unsuccessfully. "At least someone in this room agrees with me on that point." His smile disappeared as Jole shot him a hard look.

Jenneane looked from one man to the other in dismay. "He kissed me," she explained.

Tirin scowled. "And followed you when you didn't want his company. And wouldn't release you when you ordered him to. And ripped—" His jaw was tight in barely leashed fury.

His daughter turned on Tirin with an expression of dismay. "You're not helping matters," Jenneane warned him.

Tirin leaned down until he was nearly nose to nose with her, seemingly forgetting Jole's presence. "Do I care? I wanted to see Byen dead from the first. Only the fact that his head belonged to your father stopped—"

"Enough." Jole put up a hand for silence.

Tirin and Jenneane glanced at him as if suddenly remembering his interrogation of them.

"Actually, I rather appreciate Captain Tirin's candor in this matter." Jole sighed.

Byen would have to pay the ultimate price for this. Jole hated to do it, but he had two other daughters to protect, and it couldn't seem that he would let any trespass of this nature go unanswered.

Tirin bowed his head slightly. "Thank you, Majesty."

"You are not clear of my wrath yet."

He nodded grimly.

"Why didn't you turn Byen over to Panor

immediately?"

He shot a look of supplication skyward.

Jenneane shifted uncomfortably. "Tirin was too busy arguing my choice and keeping me safe."

"And?" Jole prodded. It was clear they'd done more than make their way back to her rooms.

"That was my fault. I pursued Tirin. I left my rooms tonight to find him."

"Really?" Jole drawled, raising an eyebrow in disbelief.

Jenneane met his eyes steadily, challenging him.

Tirin cleared his throat. "I wasn't a complete innocent in the matter, as you well heard."

"I heard very well," Jole snapped without looking away from his daughter's face. "What did you think you were doing?"

Jenneane's eyes widened. "You said you'd allow me any man I chose," she whispered. "Please, Father. Tirin is the only man I want, the only man I've ever—"

Jole nodded slowly, an idea taking form. "If the contract is acceptable," he conceded.

"You'd really use non-allowance?" Tears filled her eyes.

"To protect your rights, I would."

Tirin nodded. "I ask nothing if I dissolve. I offer... What do you want, Jenneane?"

She hesitated. "I want you."

"Fidelity?" He nodded. "You know I offer that." Tirin glanced at Jole nervously. "Name your stipulations. Anything you ask."

Jole took in Tirin's earnest expression and the tears in Jenneane's eyes. He sighed. He would know the true measure of the man shortly. For Jenneane's sake, he hoped Tirin was the right sort of man. It would crush her, if he was not.

"Fidelity from each of you. In a split, the children reside with Jenneane, no matter who dissolves. No property split. Neither of you will gain by dissolving the contract." Jole expected shock from Tirin, a proclamation that he deserved compensation if Jenneane was the one to dissolve the contract.

Tirin smiled widely. "Then we have your permission to contract?" he asked, visibly relieved.

"You would sign that contract?"

"Tirin, no," Jenneane whispered. "You can't—"

"This moment, if I had it in front of me," Tirin responded solemnly.

"Tomorrow morning, when my magistrate arrives. I had contracts prepared a year ago, in preparation for this day."

"Thank you, Majesty."

Jole slid from the bed. "I suppose you'll be calling me Jole now."

Tirin nodded uncertainly. "Jole." He tried out the name, testing how readily he could call it to his tongue.

Jenneane stood on tiptoe and kissed her father's cheek. "Thank you, *Daddy*," she whispered.

Jole nodded, touched at her use of the baby term her mother had taught her. Jenneane hadn't called him that in at least five years. "You know I simply want you to be happy."

"I know."

Tirin dropped a kiss on Jenneane's temple. "In

the morning," he promised her. He motioned for Jole to precede him to the door.

Jole bit back a grin. Tirin would actually leave her to make Jole happy or keep up appearances. "The contract is accepted. It appears that I interrupted a rather delicate moment, and I remember how frustrating that can be.

"Casual clothing will be delivered for you. I will expect a contract signed at breakfast. I would advise you not to be late, and both of you should bathe before then.

"Oh...Tirin. One of our woman healers will be stationed in the hall in a few moments to oversee the traditional first mating. I will...overlook this oversight, in consideration of your mating frenzy. I trust you will take more care for such things, in the future."

Tirin swallowed hard, and Jenneane covered a wide-mouthed look of surprise with a shaking hand.

"Am I understood, Tirin?" He put the edge of an order in that question.

The captain nodded. "Yes, Maj—"

Jole glared at him.

"Yes, Jole. We'll sign the contract at breakfast, and I will be more mindful in the future."

"Try not to be late." He sighed.

Jenneane blushed as Jole closed the door behind him. He smiled widely. They'd be late, but it was good that they would.

* * * *

Jenneane stood, staring at the door in shock. She'd expected a much different outcome when her father met them with such hostility.

"Did he just...?" Tirin breathed.

She nodded. "Yes. I think he did."

He wrapped an arm around her, snuggling his body to hers. "Are you all right?"

Jenneane relaxed into the hard muscles of his chest. "In your arms? How could I be anything but?"

Tirin chuckled against Jenneane's throat, moving his hand to her mound and pressing her to the hard ridge of his cock.

"Did you have an erection the entire time my father was here?" she teased.

"With you half dressed and pressed to my body? Not even your father could kill my arousal."

"I won't tell him, if you don't."

Tirin's lips stroked her shoulder. He backed away a step and started unhooking her outfit again.

Jenneane gasped.

He stilled. "Nervous?"

She laughed. "A bit."

"Would you rather wait until—"

Jenneane turned to him. "I want you, Tirin. Please don't stop."

He cast her a hungry look. "Lower your arms."

She dropped her arms to her side, and the bodice of her costume slid after them. Tirin smiled, taking her hands one at a time and removing the sleeves from them. When he was finished, the bodice pooled at her hips.

Tirin panned his gaze over her body. "I was

wrong."

"Wrong?" Jenneane resisted the urge to cover herself. Was he pleased with what he saw? Or was something amiss?

"I thought that costume couldn't possibly hide anything. I was wrong."

Her breathing was harsh in her own ears. The touch of his gaze was like a physical caress. "What is it hiding?"

He cupped a breast, his expression fiercely possessive. "You are unlike any woman on Kegin. Your nipples are a color between pink and tan instead of choc."

Jenneane moaned as his fingers danced over that nipple, teasing it to a rigid peak. "It's—my human genes," she explained in something akin to a pant.

Tirin's hands moved to the last of the hooks, opening them quickly and efficiently. "What other secrets does this silin hide from me?"

"The doctors—"

He kissed her—a hot, hard kiss. "No. Let me discover the differences."

Jenneane nodded her agreement, kicking off her boots as his hands pushed the fabric from her hips. She hoped he would like the differences.

Tirin dropped to one knee, laying a kiss on her curls as he eased the costume down her thighs. "You smell sweet...spicy. You smell like Cimmeg implin cakes covered in warm sucre. You know that is the lovers' repast?"

Jenneane nodded. "On the contract night. For a first mating," she corrected herself. *And the mother's fast—and any other time the lovers want to live the tradition.*

He balanced her as he removed first one leg of the costume and then the other. Tirin shot another of those hungry looks her way. "Order some." It wasn't a request or even a suggestion.

She licked her lips, frowning in confusion. "Lovers' repast?"

He nodded.

Her mouth quirked in amusement. "To make my father wonder, or so I won't grow faint in my virginal fragility beneath your masculine lusts?" she quoted Syl's instruction. "Though my woman healer believes that women are incapable of experiencing all the levels of delight in a first mating without succumbing to it completely, I don't share her viewpoint that all women are so weak." Jenneane wasn't a fragile flower. The thought was ridiculous.

"You will order it, because it would delight me to compare your flavors to the culinary treat—and to make your father near mad in the knowledge that he has left you to satisfy those urges."

Jenneane gulped as his meaning became clear. Her mother and Syl had told her men drank at a woman's body sometimes as a form of love play. She hadn't expected it tonight. "You want to taste me?" she asked weakly.

"Do you deny that you are mine to taste?" he countered archly, rising to tower over her.

She shook her head, unable to form words.

Tirin touched her weeping core, growling in satisfaction at her readiness for his first possession. Jenneane shivered as he brought his fingertips to his tongue. His eyes closed in ecstasy.

He opened them again. "Order the lovers' repast, Jenneane."

She glanced at her naked form and headed for her cabinet to get a silin robe. Tirin was there first, holding the door closed with one large hand.

"I can't speak to the guards undressed like this," she whispered. He couldn't mean that.

Tirin pulled off his jacket and dropped it to the floor. He dragged his tunic off his broad shoulders and pulled it over her head. "A sign that you are mine," he explained.

Jenneane pushed her arms into the sleeves and smoothed the fabric over her thighs, his musk enveloping her. Her nipples hardened to tiny peaks that drew his gaze. She ran her fingers over the dark curls on Tirin's chest, tracing the line to the waistband of his trousers.

"Order the food, Jenneane, before I forget myself and your pleasure in my lust." He growled the warning, standing back and motioning her to the door.

She went to it and pulled it open, fully aware of Tirin's eyes on her body. "Lieutenant?" she called, pulling the open ties closed over her breasts.

The soldier turned to her, and his eyes widened in shock. His gaze shifted away, then lowered toward the floor. He paled. "Yes, Highness?"

Jenneane didn't have to look at him to know that Tirin was issuing a silent threat of death to the soldier. "Lovers' repast, please, Gi."

Tirin's voice rumbled at her ear, his hands caressing her stomach in a blatant show of possession, of his right to touch her when the soldier dared not look at her. His words took a moment to sink in.

"You have a quarter of an hour, Lieutenant," he growled. "I know the kitchen will have lovers' repast prepared for nights like this. Go quickly."

The soldier bowed. "Yes, sir."

Tirin closed the door, then stripped his tunic from her body. Jenneane had barely caught her breath before she found herself laid on the silin sheets of her bed. He pulled her thighs wide and knelt between them.

"Now we will see what you've hidden from me." Tirin pulled the clip from Jenneane's hair, spreading it over the pillow beneath her head. "Your hair is softer than silin," he breathed. "I want to feel your hair on my chest and in my hands as I take you."

Jenneane nodded, her body weak in tremors of need.

"I love looking at your naked body."

"Do more than look," she pleaded, reaching for the choker to complete the disrobing.

"No," Tirin ordered.

Her hands stilled, and she stared at him, confused.

"I have plans for the choker. Next time. Nothing makes me harder than seeing you in nothing but that piece of jewelry."

"Plans?" Jenneane whispered, her body heating at the insinuation, at the possibilities of being educated by this man.

"Next time." His gaze moved down her body. "Your lips are so pale and delicate but lush from my kisses."

Tirin did kiss her, an urgent kiss that demanded all her passion, that poured his back to her until she felt she might actually faint in pleasure. Jenneane pulled at the buttons on his trousers, popping the top three and baring the head of his cock. He pulled her hand away, a smug smile making his face seem all the more dangerous and exciting.

"Enough," Tirin decided. "That is enough to make my intent clear to that upstart lieutenant. Any more and your pleasure will be compromised."

His mouth moved to her breasts, teasing her quickly to a mindless response and moving on, down her stomach to her curls.

"All your hair is so rich...deep red undertones in the choc curls." Tirin spread her thighs wider, his eyes glazed in desire. "Your sex is pale as your lips, pink and perfect, tiny and so ready for me."

Jenneane arched up to his mouth as Tirin licked at her seam. She felt that touch through her whole body, as if his tongue caressed her breasts and neck, her stomach and thighs all at once. "Please, Tirin," she begged. Jenneane would give anything for more of him.

"Your taste sets me on fire. I want to taste you for the rest of my life."

"I want more," she pleaded.

Tirin's tongue flicked inside her.

Jenneane cried out harshly. *Fire.* Wildfire shot over every nerve in her body. She tipped her hips, offering herself fully to Tirin, then sobbed at a hesitant knock at the door.

He eased back, his chin coated in her honey, and nuzzled his face in her curls to dry himself. Tirin pulled a quilt over her, then stalked to the door, his muscles rippling, making a powerful show. Jenneane gasped in the realization that he fully intended to take the tray with his trousers half-open.

Tirin's state of undress wasn't lost on the lieutenant. The younger man darkened, shaking as he turned his face away to the corridor. It was clearly a challenge, a warning Tirin was issuing not simply to the lieutenant but to every man on Kegin.

The lieutenant passed the test. He kept his eyes down and his face averted. His gaze didn't so much as flick toward Jenneane on the bed.

She warmed. No man would dare paw at her, undress her with his eyes, or make inappropriate suggestions as long as Tirin lived.

Tirin bowed to someone and then turned with the tray in his hands, revealing a flash of Syl in the hall, prepared to care for her in case Jenneane reacted badly to her first stimulation, fulfilling the ancient tradition without comment as she'd known she would from the day Jenneane was born.

Was he thanking Syl for her service? It seemed the thoughtful type of thing Tirin would do.

He closed the door, offering Jenneane an expression that promised no more interruptions to his sweet torture of her. He set the tray on the bedside table, then stripped off his trousers and boots.

Jenneane moved her gaze over him slowly.

She picked up one of the cakes from the tray and took a bite, offering the next bite to Tirin in the formal manner Syl had trained her for. A Keen man would expect the symbolic sharing of sweetness, before their intimacy to strengthen Jenneane for the mating to come...and after to rejuvenate her from the ordeal.

He shook his head, guiding her hand back to the tray. "Not yet," he growled.

She looked at the tray in confusion, all Syl's instruction failing her in the moment Jenneane needed it most. "But, tradition—"

Tirin pulled the quilt away, his cock pulsing as his gaze moved over her. He knelt between her thighs. "We will have the cakes...but only after I accomplish two things."

"Two?" she gasped. Only one task came readily to mind.

"Two," he assured her. "The first is the comparison I wanted."

He pulled the flask of heated sucre sap from the tray. The cakes were already drizzled with the sap, of course, but more was placed in the flask. Jenneane had always assumed it was there for dipping the cakes into, an added rush of carbohydrates. Watching Tirin pull the cork, she wondered if other lovers had played the game he intended, if this was a ritual that she had no knowledge of. That was unlikely, which meant Tirin had devised this torture for her especially.

"And?" Jenneane prayed he would lay claim to her properly then. His love play was likely to kill her with pleasure otherwise.

Tirin set the cork aside on the tray. "I'm not

going to stop until you're faint and in need of their restorative properties."

He'll kill me with pleasure. A fresh wave of her personal lubricant accompanied that realization. Jenneane leaned back on her elbows, in need of a feeling of being grounded.

She jerked as Tirin spread her sex and dripped the thick, warm sucre over her hood and along her inner seam. Her muscles tightened and her breathing hitched as he lowered his head.

Tirin sucked the sap from her hood, groaning at her throaty cry of pleasure. He moved to her sex, diligently chasing each droplet. Jenneane shivered, as he cleaned her perineum, surprised at how arousing his mouth was, no matter where he touched her. As if proving her belief, Tirin's tongue rasped over the puckered opening of her anus, stealing the last of the sucre from her body. Jenneane screamed, at the edges of control.

She reached for Tirin. Her body craved that final completion she'd only heard of and dreamed of, the moment when Tirin's cock would engorge and lock into the stim band at the entrance to her womb, the moment when she would release her first egg and her gates would open wide and draw in his seed.

His tongue darted deep in her. She felt an orgasm crash over her, much more powerful than her self-release. Breath-stealing, it set her senses in a spin. Jenneane met Tirin's eyes as he looked up in surprise. She couldn't form words, and she couldn't fathom what she'd say if she could speak. Jenneane sank to the bed slowly.

Tirin rose up over her with a muttered curse.

"Too fast," he growled, dropping the flask onto the tray. It clinked, tipped, landed on its side with a light click, spilling its thick cargo over the metal surface unheeded.

The head of his cock spread her entrance wide. "Tell me what you want, Jenneane."

She closed her eyes. Tirin took her beyond the soul's reward and expected her to speak?

"Now, Jenneane. While your body is lost in pleasure," he demanded. "I cannot take you, unless you—"

Jenneane threw her hips up, encasing Tirin in her sheath. He forced his body further, shivering as her barrier crumbled to his thrust. She cried out in a combination of pain and pleasure, knowing instinctively the pleasure still to come, the pleasure that Tirin would give her.

He stilled, his entire body trembling as he smoothed her hair. "It will pass," Tirin promised. "Open for me."

Jenneane rocked her hips to him, desperate for full completion, for the second pleasure that would make her whole—or shatter her foundations. Suddenly, the thought that Tirin could shatter her wasn't so unbelievable.

"Yes," he hissed.

Tirin took her in strong, deep strokes, his body driving her further, to the edges of reason. Jenneane gasped as his seed filled her. His groan caressed her raw senses.

"Take me," Tirin pleaded. "Take all of me."

He lodged his cock deep and swelled. The head bit her waiting band. Jenneane screamed in pleasure as his hips pressed her hard to the bed.

Her gates opened, and the heat of his seed poured through into her womb.

The shocks of her ovum sacs contracting to release an egg stole her breath. Jenneane heard Tirin chuckle as her world went dark.

CHAPTER SIX

Jenneane groaned at the pleasure that seemed never to end. Realization came slowly. She was upright, cradled to Tirin's chest. His index and ring fingers spread her core wide for his middle finger to massage her inner pleasure spot. She gasped, her body tensing for another release. Jenneane tried to close her legs, to deny the call of another shattering release that she felt might truly kill her, but his body kept her spread wide.

"Tirin, I can't," she whimpered.

"You can. You must come for me."

"I have." *Twice.* "I fainted?" she asked, mortified in the realization that she must have. After the many times she'd argued with Syl that she wasn't weak, she'd fainted.

"Yes." His voice was self-satisfied. His finger grew more insistent.

Jenneane threw her head back, screaming his name as the waves of pleasure took her again. A wash of her musk flooded over his hand, forced out by her inner contractions. Tirin growled a curse. His cock, hard again, touched her thigh, demanding attention she was too tired to give.

"Perfect," Tirin decided, laughing lightly.

"Perfect?" she panted out, confused by that pronouncement.

He lowered her to the pillows gently, easing his hand from her. Tirin brushed silin against her spasming center, exciting the area already painfully sensitized from his loving. Jenneane twisted beneath him, pleading for Tirin to let her recover, trying to escape the mixed pleasure and agony of the silin stroking her.

"Please stop. I can't... I can't..." Gods! But, her body wanted to even now.

Tirin grinned and removed the top sheet from beneath her gently. "It is done," he soothed her. He stood with the sheet draped over his arm, pulled a quilt to cover her, and brushed a kiss along her lips.

"Done?" she repeated in a thick, exhausted voice, curling to her side.

He nodded, folding the sheet carefully.

Jenneane furrowed her brow. "What are you doing?"

"Sending the proof of a maiden bride to your father," Tirin explained patiently.

Her exhaustion fled. "That hasn't been done in centuries," she protested.

Jenneane felt a deep blush come up. *He had to make me climax again to force a sufficient amount of my maiden's blood out of me. Tirin didn't pull out as the barrier broke to collect the proof then.* "This isn't necessary."

By the ancient tradition, an untried bride was highly valued. In the first era of the schaen, it was unusual for a high-noble or royal female to make the years between fifteen and twenty intact to a contract.

In cases where the bride was believed virginal, before the contract was sealed, the male was given a night with his bride. The bed sheets were delivered to the bride's father. If her barrier blood stained them, the husband had the bragging rights of claiming his maiden bride but he owed five hundred gold coin to the bride's father when the contract was signed. If there was no blood, the contract would go on, but the father of the bride owed an equal sum to the new husband. If the father...or sometimes the husband chose, he could display the stained sheets as proof of the bride's virtue to the contract bed.

Tirin bit back a laugh. "It is necessary. There will be no question that I have been your first, that...I will be the only man you take." He faltered, shooting her an uncertain glance.

Jenneane smiled at the sentiment. "I want you, Tirin. I'll never want another. What other man could make me faint in pleasure? But... Mag alive! Five hundred gold coins for that small satisfaction?"

He placed the sheet on the edge of the bed, the pink-red stain prominently displayed on top. Tirin sat beside her, taking her hand and planting a kiss in the palm. "You are worth a thousand times that much if you truly want me."

She sighed. "After a rest?" she teased. Jenneane did want him, but her entire body ached from his loving.

Tirin raised an eyebrow. "We will eat our lovers' repast and bathe. If you don't fall asleep, we'll see what you are ready for. For now, I'll deliver the proof of maiden bride to our young envoy."

"Do me one favor, Tirin."

"Anything for you, love."

"Don't do this in the nude."

He laughed heartily. "A towel?" he offered.

"Fair enough."

* * * *

Joseph stared at his father's smirk suspiciously. Jole had been gone for well over an hour, and his return was unannounced.

"Is there any news?" Susan asked urgently.

Jole nodded. "Jenneane is in her room, and she's fine."

Joseph sighed in relief.

Panor marched into the office, nodding his head to Jole. "I sent the men off to their duties or beds, as you ordered. Should I send Lord Byen away or—"

His father's face hardened. "Lock him in a cell until I decide what to do with him. I may let him rot for a week or so before I bother with him."

Joseph groaned in the realization that Byen must have injured Jenneane. *Why didn't I go after her when I saw Byen following her?*

Panor shook his head in confusion. "You won't be giving him a ritual death?" he asked.

Jole's throat bobbed as if he bit back a laugh. "I haven't decided yet."

"What is there to decide?" Joseph insisted. *If Father won't do it, I will. As an adult brother, I can offer Jenneane assurances as well as our father can.*

Jole arched an eyebrow at his bride. "I may decide to let her husband do the honors. He would dearly love to finish what he started in the garden."

"Her what?" Joseph thundered. *Dear Mag! What went on tonight?*

"Who?" Panor inquired, looking ready for battle.

Susan doubled in relieved laughter.

Jole joined her. "Jenneane left her rooms to seek out her mate. She will be contracting with Captain Tirin in the morning. Panor, I will need you to contact my magistrate and tell him to bring the necessary documents."

Panor departed with a grumbled, "As you wish."

Joseph sighed in relief. "I know Tirin." He made an effort to know as many of the lords vying for his sister's hand as he could. "He's a good man." *Much better than Byen, by far.*

Susan sank to a chair. "He agreed to the contract we wanted?"

Jole laughed heartily. "He agreed to less. Tirin agreed to sign away every right he has to her."

"You wouldn't," she protested.

"Of course not. The contract stands. If Jenneane dissolves the contract, Tirin will have an ample penalty. I don't think it matters to him, but he'll have it."

Joseph rubbed his forehead in disbelief as their conversation went on. He never guessed Jenneane would find a mate in such a whirlwind manner. It made his own waiting seem endless.

A guard knocked at the door, looking decidedly miserable. "Majesty?"

Jole turned to him. "Yes, Lieutenant?"

The man's hands shook as he offered a white silin bundle to the king.

"And the meaning of this?" Jole asked with an arched eyebrow.

"Captain Tirin offers proof of a maiden bride, Majesty. Payment will exchange at the signing. I know this is an ancient custom, but Tirin felt it was appropriate to offer."

Jole chuckled as he accepted the blood and semen soaked sheets that proved Jenneane was Tirin's bride—and not an untried virgin any longer. "Very well, Lieutenant. You may go."

Joseph blushed. "I'll leave you to it," he decided. Seeing the evidence of his twin's success was not to his tastes...or good for his sanity.

He left his father's office and headed to his rooms, feeling happy for Jenneane but oddly bereft. Perhaps because Jenneane no longer shared his plight.

Joseph paused at the foot of the stairs to glance at Berel in longing across the entry hall. Syl's daughter wouldn't be of age for more than two more years, and she would resist the idea of being Joseph's mate when she was old enough to be his.

Berel noticed him and offered a wide smile and a wave.

Joseph managed a strained smile in return, turning up the stairs before he could do something illegal to lay claim to her.

It would be a long two years, but Joseph would wait for Berel for a decade if he had to. He'd already waited a year for her. How much worse could two more be?

Berel would be his. Joseph had been promised any willing woman he wished. Noble or not,

Joseph wanted Berel. She was his dearest friend—and Jenneane's. Berel knew his heart and mind better than anyone did, better than his twin...except for this one thing. Jenneane knew how he wanted Berel, but his chosen bride was seemingly unaware of the fact. Joseph had wanted her since he was fifteen and Berel a budding twelve. In a world full of willing women, Joseph wanted the one woman he would have to convince.

CHAPTER SEVEN

Abrin 35th, Ri 25-3008

"Stop, Tirin." Jenneane giggled, pushing his hands away. "My father—"

"Doesn't actually expect us to be on time," he chided her, his eyes playful.

Tirin slid his fingertips through the slit in her Earth-style dress, a wrapped design that Susan favored. The dress had had his undivided attention since Jenneane had put it on. So different from the typical Keen style of dress, Tirin had insisted on examining it before Jenneane wore it into the corridors.

"Mag alive," he groaned. "This is positively indecent." His fingers stroked her hood, urging her legs further apart for his play.

Jenneane leaned her head to his chest, gasping as Tirin's fingers breached her body. "You wish me to change my clothes?" she asked.

"No. I wish you to wear a dress like this every day." His voice was strained. "Your breasts invite me, and your sweet sheath..." He untied the waist and swept the dress open, a smile curving the dark line of his lips.

"Every day?" Jenneane managed, mentally calculating the time it would take the clothier to arrange that. She fisted his tunic in her hands as Tirin played at her inner pleasure spot, his free hand pulling his trousers open.

Tirin tipped her chin up, tugging at the choker

to draw Jenneane's face closer to his. His mouth closed over hers.

Jenneane shivered in the memory of her complete surrender to Tirin through the night. All her training as a princess meant nothing in the face of him. Tirin ordered her and rewarded every act of obedience handsomely. And she reveled in his possession.

"Every day." He nipped at her lips. "Until they don't fit you anymore."

"Fit?" *Why would the dresses not fit anymore?*

Tirin lifted her, impaling Jenneane on his length again. He pressed her to the wall, supporting her thighs on his forearms, thrusting inside her in yet another show of possession that she loved.

"Soon," he whispered. "Very soon, you will carry my child."

She whimpered, knowing Tirin was right about that, knowing he would make certain that it happened just as he foretold. Her body reached for the climax of her egg releasing, the heat of his seed flooding her womb.

"You want that," he continued, his mouth exploring her face while his cock worked furiously to make his heir a reality. Tirin didn't question that she wanted to conceive.

He didn't have to question it. The scream of delight that tore from Jenneane's throat was answer enough. Her body spasmed around him, preparing to drink in his essence.

"Now, please," she begged. His name left her lips as a howl as Tirin pinned her tight to the wall, the head of his cock lodged against the gates of her womb.

"Now," he agreed hoarsely, bringing his mouth down on hers.

Tirin's cock pulsed inside her, a rush of heat stroking over the gates of her womb. He thickened, locking into her stim band as the force of his continuing climax sent the hot wave deep into her womb, the gates open wide for its advance, mixing with the shocks of her releasing egg until they felt one and the same. Their kiss was fevered, Jenneane meeting him even more avidly than she had the night before.

When Tirin lessened inside her, he smiled and stroked her cheek, pleased as always with the strength of her responses to him.

Jenneane blushed, fumbling with the ties on her dress. She glanced to the clock, noting that they were more than a quarter of an hour late for breakfast.

Tirin shook his head, then laid a kiss on her cheek. "He doesn't expect us on time. It is our first morning together. Relax." His hands circled her waist slowly, and he offered Jenneane another hungry look.

Her body throbbed for him. Jenneane gasped in surprise. Tirin was insatiable, and so—it seemed—was she. He groaned as her inner muscles gripped and released his length, the mere hint that he wanted her again while he lay buried in her sending Jenneane over.

She met his eyes, drinking in the stark need in them. Jenneane breathed deeply of their mixed musk, reaching to lick at the pulse point at his throat, gathering his taste and firing the already heady arousal coursing through her.

"That's right," he crooned. Tirin eased Jenneane off of his length and set her on her feet.

"No," she pleaded. What was he doing? He couldn't leave her in this state.

Tirin smiled a smug little smile and fastened his trousers. He smoothed her dress, taking great care, stroking his fingers down her thighs and over the bodice, sensitizing her abdomen and breasts further.

"Tirin?"

"When the contract is signed and we have eaten," he assured her.

"But," she began. Jenneane faltered at a brisk knock at the door.

"Jenneane," Joseph called out. "The magistrate is waiting. And so is Father." That last held a note of warning.

Jenneane grimaced at that. Why had she let Tirin talk her into making love again that morning?

Tirin chuckled, placing her hand on his crooked arm. "Your father is so predictable," he mused.

She raised an eyebrow, praying he was reading Jole better than she was. "Really? He surprised you last night," she challenged, matching his stride toward the door and her waiting twin.

* * * *

Tirin nodded to Jole and Susan as he guided

Jenneane to the table.

The queen smiled warmly, motioning a welcome to her table that put Tirin instantly at ease. He'd heard that Susan Rig was a kind and gracious woman, but in truth, Tirin had been more frightened of her reaction than her husband's.

Jole was a Keen male, despite his re-bred roots. The king would understand exactly what Tirin meant by every aggressive stance he took regarding his bride. Susan was Earth-born, and her understanding of a sexual Keen male was limited to her husband. If any of Jenneane's family balked at him, Tirin feared it would be the queen.

Jole looked to the clock pointedly. "I believe I suggested you make it here on time," he offered, a slight tension in his jaw.

The younger prince sniggered over his breakfast.

Tirin laughed. "Did you come to breakfast at your normal time after your first night with your bride?" he asked boldly. It wasn't a question asked in polite society, but this was a thinly-veiled civility, a challenge of Tirin as a strong enough mate for a Keen princess. It wasn't a challenge Tirin intended to lose.

Jole tried to hide a smile at that. Tirin had passed that test. He only wondered how many more tests would come before he signed the contract that bound Jenneane to him.

Susan sighed and rolled her eyes. "No. We didn't leave the bed, and breakfast was brought to us. Now stop."

81

Tirin laughed heartily at that, and Jole joined him. Jenneane shook her head, a bright smile lighting her green eyes. Joseph looked a trifle uncomfortable at the entire conversation, glancing toward the kitchens as if looking for the arrival of something of interest.

Jole recovered first. "Well, now that my bride has ruined any chance I had of acting the part of a proper Keen father—"

"Oh, please just let them sit," Susan snapped. "Stop being a Keen king long enough to permit our daughter and her husband to eat."

Tirin eased Jenneane's chair in to the table, beating Joseph to the task with only a moment to spare. Joseph darkened, nodding as he relinquished what Tirin would assume was his accustomed place at his sister's side. Tirin dropped down beside her, casting his gaze about the table at the other two princesses. Though it hardly seemed possible, the two looked even more human than Jenneane did. He nodded to them in turn and glanced back toward Joseph, surprised to see that he had left the room.

Before he could question her brother's disappearance, servants started setting plates of food before Tirin and Jenneane. He nodded his thanks, suddenly ravenous. Tirin smiled at the thought that he intended to work them both to hearty appetites as often as his bride would allow.

For several minutes, the royal family fell into near silence, broken only by the occasional pleasantry and the sounds of eating. Jenneane's younger siblings looked at Tirin often, as if they wished to ask him many questions but felt it rude to interrupt his first meal with the family.

"Father," Joseph called from the doorway. "We have matters to attend to."

"Of course. Show them in," Jole answered, not pausing at his enjoyment of his meal. He was a true Keen king.

Joseph tipped his head only slightly and motioned to someone in the corridor, then strode to his seat, just as a servant placed his plate before him. He spared not a moment's notice to the activity around them, trained well for his place as future king.

"Them?" Jenneane asked. "Your magistrate and who—" She made it no further.

A shrill voice carried into the cavernous room, answering her half-asked question. "I demand to know what is being done," Giriam demanded. "I would think royal guards would be more competent than this."

"Yes, mi'lady," a gruff voice answered with the minimum of respect due a lady of Giriam's place.

Jenneane's eyes widened. Tirin grimaced and then nodded. Yes, as she guessed, it was his mother.

"Oh, Your Majesty," Giriam simpered. "I just don't know what to think." She fell into a stunned silence as Tirin turned to face her. Giriam recovered quickly, just as Tirin knew she would. "Tirin! Oh, I am *so* pleased."

"I'm certain you are," Tirin managed dryly. *Not so much to find me alive as to find me in the hospitality of the royal family this early in the day.*

"Where have you been all night? Are you well?"

"Everything is fine, Mother." He hesitated, shooting a pained look at Jenneane. As much as Tirin wanted to shout his triumph to the stars, his bride knew better than anyone how he hated to give his mother her coveted prize.

Jenneane urged him on with a nod.

Tirin sighed and met Giriam's eyes again. "I was arranging a contract," he motioned to Jenneane, "with my bride and her family."

A sly smile flirted with his mother's lips. "I see. I will send for our magistrate at once and—"

"You will not," Tirin growled, shooting her a warning look.

"It would be expected that the expense of a match with a re-bred—"

"I've seen that contract. I won't permit Jenneane to sign it."

Jole raised an eyebrow in surprise at Tirin's candor—or perhaps at the audacity of Tirin ordering a Keen princess, even one who would be his wife.

Giriam blanched. "The contract is fair," she protested.

"It's an insult. It makes me little better than a stud paid for his services."

"Tirin," she gasped.

Tirin took Jenneane's hand. "Jole and I have made our own agreement. That is the contract I intend to sign."

Jole cleared his throat, red faced. "I wouldn't have asked you to sign that."

Tirin swallowed a laugh. "You were testing me?"

"Well," Jole hedged, looking highly

discomfited.

"Yes," Susan snapped. "It was a horrible thing to do. The actual contract favors you much more."

Tirin raised Jenneane's hand and kissed it lightly. "It doesn't have to, but I thank you for your kindness."

Jenneane blushed, the intriguing pink that stained her fair skin. She shot a bashful look at her parents and met his eyes again.

"Very well," Giriam commented, hiding her fury studiously. "If there is anything else you require—"

"There is," Tirin informed her. "I'll need five hundred gold coins in the next hour—and some of my clothing later today."

"Five hundred?" she stormed.

Tirin nodded.

"Whatever for?"

"For my maiden bride. The agreement was made."

"If it—" Jole began.

Tirin favored him with a quelling look. "It will be a matter of public record, if you please."

He nodded. "As you wish." Jole shot his daughter a questioning look.

Jenneane shrugged. "Tirin wants no doubts—no rumors."

Tirin nodded. There were rumors. He knew there were, and he'd kill the man who started them when he found the culprit responsible.

"As you wish," Giriam sighed. "I'll send your things along." She turned to leave.

"Thank you, Giriam Laes," Jenneane called after her. "For raising Tirin to be an honorable man."

His mother looked back in surprise. "Would you consider visiting our home—from time to time?" she asked nervously.

"Of course. Perhaps your servant could take a few of my things back with him when he brings Tirin's here."

Tirin smiled. It was an inspired move. His mother would be mollified by her agreement.

Giriam bowed her head with a smile that announced her plans for this new alliance with the royal family. Before long, he and Jenneane would be invited to any number of events his mother planned to flaunt this association.

CHAPTER EIGHT

Veril 4th, Ri 25-3008

Tirin turned from the door with a scowl on his face. He'd been lost in bliss with Jenneane for six days, both here at the palace and at his mother's home, completely forgetting the more practical side of their union—and of their meeting.

"What is it?" Jenneane asked, pulling her thick braid back with combs in preparation for their ride together.

He folded the note into the pocket of the red and gold jacket that Jole had delivered to him that morning. It was a sign of his place as a mate to the king's daughter that Tirin should wear the royal colors now. "Our ride will have to wait for a bit. I will return shortly."

She stilled, confusion clouding her bright eyes. "Tirin?"

"Your father sent for me," he admitted.

"Is there a problem?" she asked urgently.

"More like...unfinished business between us."

"Of what sort?"

He met her eyes, dreading the argument about to start between them. Jenneane took his lead sexually, but she was not accustomed to being ordered in other areas of her life, and in truth, he loved the balance of fire and submission in her. "It's time to deal with Byen."

All color drained from her face. "No. Please don't. You've won. You have proof of—of everything you wanted proof of. Isn't that enough?"

Tirin resisted the urge to snap at her. It wasn't enough. Six days in a prison cell weren't nearly enough punishment for what Byen had tried to do to Jenneane. Without Tirin's interference, Byen might have forced himself on her, and visions of that might drive him truly mad.

He shook his head slowly, reining in his fury. "No. It's not."

"Why not?" she demanded. "He doesn't dare touch me now."

"He shouldn't have dared touch you then," he grumbled. Tirin crossed to her and took Jenneane's hands in his, sighing.

"Please, Tirin." Tears filled her eyes.

"The choice is out of my hands. Even if I don't—Your father will kill him. If he didn't, Joseph would. I dare say young Pyter would, if he were old enough to give assurances."

"Why? I don't understand why," she decided miserably.

"You have two younger sisters," he reminded her.

"You think Byen is stupid enough to wager his life again?"

Tirin kissed her forehead. "Perhaps not, but if the other lords believe they can get away with it, what protection will Eve and Rebecca have?"

Jenneane shuddered. "Let my father do it. Please, let him— For me."

"As you wish, but I must attend."

"No. *We* must." Jenneane's eyes were hard in decision.

"This will not be—"

"I know, but I must do this."

Tirin shook his head. "I would prefer that you stay here...or with your mother, but if you wish to do this, I will not stand in your way."

* * * *

Jole looked up in surprise as Jenneane entered his office on Tirin's arm. "Jenneane, you shouldn't—"

Tirin waved him off. "She insists. I can't talk her out of this, and I doubt you will be able to either."

"I won't change my mind," Jole warned her.

She nodded. "I know. I understand that."

"Women don't usually attend an execution." He spoke harshly, trying to gauge her determination.

"I know," Jenneane repeated, though she glanced to her mother's seat longingly.

"Very well."

Joseph entered the room and took his place at Jole's side, rolling his eyes at Jenneane as she stubbornly strode to the other side and stood with Tirin behind her mother's empty chair. "You'd be better off in your rooms, Neane," he offered.

She nodded shakily. "Most likely," she agreed.

"Panor will have Byen here in a few moments. You have time to leave."

"No. I'll stay." She offered her twin a strained smile.

Joseph grunted his agreement.

Byen strode into the office two steps before Panor, looking entirely too self-righteous for Jole's tastes. After six days in a cell, one would think the man would realize the enormity of the situation he faced.

Byen bowed stiffly, scowling at Jenneane and Tirin. "Have you amused yourself sufficiently, Your Highness?" he drawled.

Jenneane's eyes widened in shock. "I was hardly amused," she assured him coolly.

"Weren't you?" he challenged.

"What exactly are you accusing my sister of, Byen?" Joseph demanded, his hands fisted at his sides.

"Leading me to this," he snapped.

Jenneane gripped Tirin's arm as the captain surged toward their prisoner. He shot her a look of disbelief, guiding her hands away gently.

Joseph found his voice first. "My sister had not the slightest interest in you. You followed her and forced yourself on her."

"I should have killed him immediately," Tirin growled. "Being drunk had nothing to do with your actions. You knew what you were doing."

"Playing the fool," Byen accused, glaring at Jenneane. "What made me different? Why did you make me your target?"

"Different?" Jenneane gasped, paling.

Jole grimaced at that. Tirin had apparently never told her the tales he'd told Jole, the lies that were circulating about Jenneane.

"Different," Byen offered sarcastically. "Other lords were good enough to warm your bed and—"

Panor and Joseph both scrambled to stop

Tirin as he launched for Byen's throat.

"Stop, mi'lord," Panor requested, physically holding Tirin a little more than an arm's length from his foe.

"You will not ever speak those lies again," Tirin roared.

"Tirin," Joseph ordered.

Tirin nodded, his hands fisted in warning.

Jenneane grasped her mother's chair with shaking hands, looking ill at the unfolding scene.

"Tirin," Jole managed calmly. "Is it your wish to exact Byen's punishment?"

"Who told you those lies about her?" Tirin demanded, ignoring Jole's question.

Byen shrugged. "It is common knowledge. You don't think Her Highness contented herself with schaen, do you?" He scowled. "Every lord at that ball wanted to be her next—"

Tirin got a punch past Panor and Joseph, making Jole wonder how hard the duo had tried to stop it. This one didn't knock Byen unconscious, but it did fell him.

Jole sighed. "Panor, separate them," he ordered.

Panor and Joseph guided Tirin back to Jenneane's side.

She looked to her husband in dismay. "You know it's— Why would he s-say such...h-horrid..." she stammered.

Tirin eased her to his chest. "This geela would tell any convenient lie to save his head." He looked at Jole miserably but spoke to her. "Will you go to our room now? Or to your mother? Please, go."

"No." She turned in Tirin's arms, trembling in

some strong emotion. "Who would say such awful things?" she asked Byen quietly.

Byen stopped rubbing the rising bruise on his chin to shoot her a look of disbelief. "You claim it's a lie?"

"We know it's a lie," Jole stated, adding a note of warning.

Joseph crossed his arms over his chest. "We've seen the proof that it is. We've seen the proof from the contract bed."

Byen looked at Jenneane suspiciously. "He cut her and then healed it," he theorized.

Tirin stared at him, at first dumbstruck and then with a look promising pain. "I don't possess the ability," he growled. "Very few do."

Jole leaned across his desk. "We know Jenneane was a maiden bride. What we don't know is who started circulating these lies about her." He raised an eyebrow, waiting for an answer.

Byen faltered, looking uncertain for the first time. "I don't—know. It is just one of those things one hears."

"And you believed it?" Jole wasn't letting anyone else at Byen now. The young cur had a lot to answer for.

He swallowed hard, his color fading. "I—Yes. I did. I truly did." Byen looked to Jenneane. "My ap—"

"Byen," Jole barked. "Do you believe this defense excuses you?"

"I—"

Jole didn't give him time to answer. "You attacked my daughter, a Keen princess. You forced yourself on her—as if you had a right to touch her at all. How far would you have gone? Considering how you tore at her clothing?"

Byen shook his head slowly. "I was drunk. I never intended to—"

"That is no excuse. From what I've heard, Jenneane asked you to stop. She ordered you to."

"She struck him three times, and still he persisted," Tirin muttered, his eyes hot in fury.

Byen winced at that.

Jole nodded, fighting back his anger, wishing he had asked for the specifics earlier. "This can never happen again. There is only one way for me to ensure that it doesn't."

Byen nodded, not questioning the obvious conclusion, not begging for his life.

"Is it your wish to end this man, Tirin?"

Tirin looked to Jenneane. Her hand closed on the cuff of his jacket, and her eyes pleaded with him.

He kissed her temple gently. "No. It is your right," he whispered.

Jole nodded, plucking the ceremonial sword from his desk and striding to Byen. The young lord sank to his knees and bowed his head, whispering under his breath, most likely a prayer to Mag. It was a futile prayer to ask Fion's intervention with her god-husband, when a woman had been violated or threatened.

Jenneane turned into Tirin's chest, watching the proceedings from the safety of his arms.

Jole nodded to her. "You don't have to do this. I can delay long enough to—"

"I do," she assured him.

"As you wish." Jole looked back to Byen,

flicking the switch that sent the blue blaze of the laser cauter around the blade. "May Mag show you mercy," he prayed. Typically, he would ask that Fion sway Mag to mercy, She being the goddess of mercy and He being the god of justice, but Byen had attempted to force himself on a woman. If Byen found any mercy, it would not be from Fion, the protector of women.

Jole took the killing blow without delay.

"Jenneane?" Tirin asked.

Jole raised his eyes to her. Her breathing was erratic, her entire body trembling. A sheen of sweat glistened on her skin. Jenneane met Tirin's eyes, then collapsed into his embrace.

Tirin scooped her to his chest and headed for the door. He stilled, nuzzling her cheek, a smile appearing on his face.

"What is it?" Jole asked.

"Her woman healer is...?" He waited for a name, seemingly to commit it to memory as he hadn't in his mating frenzy.

"Our healers are Syl and Berel."

"Send one to our rooms." Tirin left before Jole could question that order.

* * * *

Jenneane shifted beneath the quilts, groaning as the silin skated over her skin. A hand touched her cheek.

"Better."

Jenneane furrowed her brow. "Berel?" she whispered.

"Good. She's waking."

Waking? She tried to piece together the situation. *Byen,* her mind supplied. Her father had killed Byen and—Jenneane groaned again, lifting a hand to her face. What was wrong with her that she was constantly fainting?

"Jenneane?" Tirin called. His hand cupped her cheek, his scent teasing her senses.

Her body exploded in waves of need, and she brushed her cheek into his hand, seeking his touch.

"So hot," he murmured.

Jenneane forced her eyes open, focusing with some difficulty on Tirin's smile. "I fainted?"

He laughed. "Understandable."

"No. I am not a weak female," she complained.

"You are not a weak female," he agreed. His lips caressed hers slowly.

"But this Len-be-damned—"

"Oxykol."

She furrowed her brow. What had the toxin to do with this? "What?"

"Oxykol. The toxin built up. You don't eat very well, and you were tired last night, so we didn't make love. You took a lizor berry and olum tea this morning. Did you, perchance, have a headache?"

Jenneane gasped in understanding. The pregnancy signs were supposed to start immediately upon implantation. They *hadn't* made love, so she wouldn't have noted the failure to drop an egg. With the cold weather setting in, she'd assumed her chill was just a drop in ambient temperature. Was it possible? She looked to Berel for confirmation. "Are you sure?"

Berel smiled widely. "Certain. Your cap has formed. Your father healed you to lower your levels. You were already at a stage two reaction. You will have to learn to eat correctly and let Tirin massage you often."

Tirin nodded. "If we continue to live here, we will have healing for you. Your father and brother have offered—"

Jenneane touched his cheek. "You wouldn't mind?" she interrupted him.

He laughed heartily. "If you and our child need healing, I wouldn't dream of leaving."

She smiled. "Tirin?"

"Yes?"

"I have another need."

His smile faltered. "Cold. You need another quilt?" he asked urgently.

She shook her head.

"Food? You're hungry?"

"No."

Berel stifled a laugh and headed for the door.

Tirin looked miserably confused. "I don't understand."

Jenneane reached for the ties on his tunic. "My schen."

* * * *

Cored turned the glass in his hand, staring through the nearly colorless iri brandy and into the flames beyond. He had failed with Princess Jenneane. Simply, without a doubt, he'd failed.

The plan should have worked, It was nearly flawless, but nearly hadn't been close enough. He fisted the glass and threw it into the flames, watching the fire lick up at the charred fragments of smoky glass.

There was only one chance to reclaim his birthright, and that was a contract with one of the precious re-bred females. His family wouldn't dare refuse to acknowledge Cored then. His older brother Cullin would have no choice but to overlook his failings.

It should have been perfect, but Princess Jenneane had resorted to tactics he hadn't anticipated. Cored hadn't expected her to sneak back to the celebration in a different outfit. He hadn't expected her to latch onto the wrong man. He'd evaluated her too soon. He'd been too confident.

Cored stared into the flames, considering his options. He wouldn't forsake this plan yet. It was the only way one of the re-breds would take him to mate. It was the only way to undo his brother's treachery and regain his name.

But how would he make the plan work? He hadn't started the rumors about Jenneane, though he had to admit that they came in very handy. He could start the rumors about another re-bred if he had to, though chances were that the rumors would always abound. It was the truth of a weak male mind that it would always see wanton behavior when none might exist.

Using another of Jole Ri's daughters would mean death. Regardless, Princess Eve wasn't naïve enough to fall for his trap, and Princess

Rebecca, reliable intelligence told him, was being schooled by schaen. Neither would work to Cored's favor.

He pushed to his feet and ambled to the desk, scooping up the decanter of iri brandy as he rifled through the notations.

Michael's children? Cored swallowed a laugh, nearly choking on the mouthful of brandy he'd taken. *Not Princess Gibril!* She was the furthest thing from a suitable bride Cored could imagine.

He scowled. Kyra would have been perfect were it not for her older sister's interference. Kyra had been innocent enough, until Gibril introduced her to schaen and nearly killed Kyra in the process. The younger princess was a shattered woman now, vowing never to mate. Kyra was too uncertain a wager, and an uncertain wager had destroyed Cored's chances this time.

"Diran," he breathed, taking another swallow of the brandy. Yes. Diran was a possibility, but it was too early to gauge. She wasn't sexually mature yet. Diran might still become an outgoing personality, or she might choose schaen when her time came.

He flicked the sheet away, looking at his last possibility. Pilar wasn't a princess, but she was a re-bred, the only daughter Lord Alex and Lady Lyssa had produced. She was four months older than Diran was. Either woman meant at least seven years of patience, but Cored would wait decades to win his re-bred bride.

Cored sank to the chair at his back, scanning his eyes over the information he had on Pilar. With two older brothers and one younger, Pilar was the most protected of his possible brides, but that fact worked to his advantage as well. Pilar was shy, almost painfully so. It was unlikely that her brothers would encourage schaen in her case—or allow men to paw her.

He sank back in his chair, a wry smile twisting his lips. It was ironic. Cored was reduced to doing what Cullin feared most to regain what was stolen from him on the basis of that misguided fear. He sighed. It wasn't right. He was using people's natural inclinations to plot a meeting and marriage, but what choice had Cullin left him?

Cored looked around the small home he was barely keeping together with the stipend he got for his healing. Some months were worse than others. When the roof needed replaced, he'd resorted to selling his services to impregnate noblewomen. Cored shivered, choking down another mouthful of the brandy. He'd hoped never to have to resort to that again, but Cored would need things for his pursuit, and that meant more money than he could scrimp from his stipend.

It might be seven years, or it might be ten, but either Diran or Pilar would be Cored's bride. He stared at his fingertips, needing to forget. One of them would feel right. One of them was the one he was waiting for.

SECTION TWO: Joseph

Under a Trial Moon

CHAPTER NINE

Endl 12th, Ri 25-3010

Berel laughed over her glass of lizor berry wine. She smiled at the small gold bracelet with the crest of Fion strung from it. She was a woman now, and as such, her mother had gifted her with the traditional symbol of a trained woman healer.

The collection of guests at her Passage Party attested to her strange status. Berel was a woman healer, daughter of the royal woman healer line and of common blood, but she had been raised with the royal children and called sister by them. Many of her acquired sibs and cousins had gathered for her, taking the place of those she didn't have herself.

Gibril, as usual, was off seeking her own pleasures. For that, Berel was grateful. Now that Gibril was legally an adult, she was the lust of every young lord.

Berel spent little time with Prince Michael's children. Still, Diran had come to this celebration and embraced Berel fondly. Berel had always liked Diran most of all Michael's children.

Lord and Lady Braeden's four children had all come to share her day. The identical Alex and Andrew confused those who didn't know them well, but the fun-seeking Alex would never be able to trick Berel into mistaking him for his twin if he tried.

Pilar was a gentle beauty, almost too sheltered

for her own good. She would have to make a match someday, and that meant being surrounded by hopeful suitors.

Carter was a carefree young boy. Berel smiled, as he chased a wariken cub he was trying to train around the ballroom floor.

All of her immediate 'family' had come to her celebration.

Jenneane was already swelling with her husband's second child, and the great Colonel Tirin divided his time between following their son Terel, as the boy toddled around the room, and pampering his bride.

Eve crinkled her freckled nose under glittering green eyes and *strawberry-blond* hair, cut in a short human style not unlike the one in video likenesses of Queen Susan when she came from Earth. Of all of the re-breds of the current generation, Eve looked the most human, and she flaunted it in one of the Earth-style gowns she'd designed herself.

Rebecca pushed deep red curls off her shoulders, sketching the proceedings and smiling warmly at the younger re-breds' antics. Rebecca was a solitary soul, no less mischievous than her older sisters but rarely joining in on the group excursions that had given Panor such fits throughout their childhood, at least now that Rolin had left the palace. When Panor's son had resided within the walls, Rebecca had thrown caution to the wind more often than she did of late.

Pyter was easily as fun-seeking as Alex, but with a rare caring streak that often caused him more problems than his misdeeds. The wariken that Carter was training was one Pyter had snuck into the palace. Eve still wore a pale pink scar on her ankle from her discovery of the cub.

Berel scanned her eyes over the last table. Her mother sat in quiet conversation with Jole and Susan. She sighed, panning her gaze about in confusion. Where had Joseph disappeared to? He had attended dinner, smiling at her as she'd opened her gifts.

She chastised herself for wondering at his absence, then added another inappropriate thought to her reasons to chide herself. This was a private function. At least Berel wouldn't be forced to watch noblewomen throw themselves at Joseph on her special night, what would be the last major affair for her at the palace.

Berel had avoided public gatherings since shortly after Joseph had reached adulthood, though he'd begged her to come to them. All her adopted sibs had begged her to come. Berel was welcome at all functions, since she was a servant sister to the royals, but the sight of women—

She bit back a groan. They touched Joseph when he didn't want them. They flirted outrageously. A few had even bribed guards to sneak them to his bedroom in hopes of seducing Joseph. They'd all failed—so far, but sooner or later some pretty face would capture his heart.

Berel played at the edge of her wineglass, suddenly morose. Some *noblewoman* would capture his eye, a lord's daughter like that snob Corin...or perhaps a general's daughter.

She tipped the glass back and forth on her

fingertip. Servant sister or not, Berel could never hope to capture Joseph for herself. She was the daughter of a royal woman healer and a lowborn guard captain who had passed away the previous winter. Worse, Joseph had been raised to think of her as a sister.

Berel chided herself again. It wouldn't matter if Joseph did want her. Corin and her band of friends had made it more than amply clear that the nobility would support nothing less than the heir apparent marrying to his station. That was the last celebration Berel had attended. Watching him with other women and knowing she could never pursue him for herself was more than she could bear.

She took a deep drink of her wine, silently acknowledging that she'd had too much. Berel should be happy. It was her twentieth birthday. She was legally an adult. She could take a husband if she chose. Unfortunately, the only man Berel wanted was beyond her reach.

And so, Berel would exercise another of her options as an adult, accepting a position as a woman healer with another house. She swallowed a lump in her throat. At least that way, she wouldn't have to see Joseph take his bride, perhaps help deliver his heirs of his chosen one.

* * * *

Joseph slipped out of the hidden corridors as Berel passed him. Everything was prepared. Now he had to convince Berel he wanted more from her.

It had been a long three years, Joseph old enough to take a bride but Berel not legally an adult. It had been a three-year sentence in the darkest dungeons of Len's Underworld, but that was all ended. Berel was an adult. She would be his.

He covered her eyes, smiling as she stiffened. "*Guess who*?" he whispered the English play words from the ancient game his mother had taught them.

Berel smiled. "Is he tall and handsome?" she teased.

"Some women think so."

"Oh. Then I can't imagine who it could be." She relaxed against his chest.

"No one comes to mind?"

"No one," she assured him. Her voice was sultry, low, inviting.

His cock stirred in response. "I hear there are princes about."

"Pyter is a boy," she scoffed.

"Joseph is a man." *An aroused man, a man who wants you.*

"It can't be Joseph."

"Joseph isn't tall and handsome?"

"Oh, he is, but you said only some women would say so. There isn't a woman I know who wouldn't say so."

"Would you say so?"

Her smile widened. "No. I wouldn't."

Joseph brushed his nose in her hair, drinking in the smell of the herbs and oils she dealt in. "Then only some would say so," he breathed.

Berel shivered in his arms. "Joseph?" she asked uncertainly.

"You are beautiful."

"Only some would say so." There was a touch of bitterness she tried to hide from him.

His heart ached that she doubted herself. "It is a night steeped in tradition, both Earth and Keen."

"Is it?" She sounded breathless.

"Would you care to sample traditions with me?"

Berel drew his hands from her face and turned to face him, pressing her back to the carved Eir wood wall. There was no sign of fear in her. Berel's eyes were bright in curiosity, just as Joseph had hoped they would be. Her face was flushed, practically glowing in emotion.

"What are these traditions?" she asked.

Joseph smiled. "The Earth tradition is a simple one. You should be kissed. Would you permit me to give you that kiss?"

He held his breath, hoping Berel had never heard the actual custom. *Sweet sixteen and never been kissed.* That kiss would have been more properly given when Berel was fifteen by Keen tradition, but even when Joseph was eighteen, he'd known he didn't possess enough self-control to kiss her and walk away.

She blushed, tipping her face to his for a chaste kiss.

Joseph laced his fingers behind her neck, brushing his thumbs over her cheeks. "No," he whispered. "Not as a sister. You are a woman. The tradition is that I will kiss you as a woman should be kissed by a man."

Her eyes widened, and her blush deepened. She took a calming breath. He tested her lips with his own. She trembled.

"Would you permit me to kiss you as a man should kiss a woman?" he asked.

"Yes." She barely breathed the word against his lips, as if afraid of saying it too loud in the deserted corridor.

He reined in the urge to take her mouth in the hot, hard kiss that he craved. He'd waited for this moment a long, long time, but it was new to Berel. Joseph tilted his head to seal his mouth to hers. He explored her, teasing her lips until Berel opened for him, a tentative parting, as if she wasn't certain what he wanted of her. Joseph groaned into her mouth, stroking his tongue along hers, drinking in the taste of lizor berry wine from her.

Berel startled and pulled back, touching her lips in wonder. "A man kisses a woman like that?" she asked in a shaky voice.

She was schooled in the mechanics of lovemaking as a woman healer, but Berel was unschooled in the reality of the act. Joseph was glad that she was. He hadn't dared find a way to keep track of her actions through the years. If Berel had any experience with men, it wasn't much, just as he'd hoped.

"Yes." He dropped his gaze, afraid that he'd frightened her off before he had the chance to convince her. Joseph smiled at the sight of her nipples, beaded against the silin gown he'd had Jenneane give Berel to wear tonight.

"Is the tradition for a kiss or for the male to

teach the female?" she asked, glancing at his lips.

Joseph leaned toward her again, thanking Fion and Mag both that she seemed willing. "To teach."

Berel nodded slowly. "It is tradition," she managed.

He didn't question how dishonorable he was being by lying to her. Joseph parted her lips, reveling in the sweet wine flavor in her mouth mixed with the Cimmeg spice perfume he'd given her for her last birthday. That choice had been a mistake. The smell of Cimmeg had driven him near mad for the last year.

Berel accepted him, making tentative advances of her own, learning what she enjoyed and what he did. Her hands tangled in his tunic, and Joseph pulled her to his body. Their kiss became more heated, less controlled as he learned her tastes. Joseph threaded his fingers through her hair, needing more but afraid of pushing too far for her comfort.

She pulled away, weaving slightly. She placed a shaking hand on his chest as if to steady herself. Joseph took advantage of her unbalanced state to pull Berel to his chest. His body ached. Joseph stilled hands that longed to caress her from head to toe. She had to come to him willingly.

"How long do these lessons continue?" she whispered.

Joseph smiled. "Would you like them to continue?"

Berel nodded.

"Then come with me. You're shaking."

They had been walking for several minutes, past the kitchens and onto the back stairs, before Berel stopped, her eyes wide. "Where are we going?"

He sighed. "My rooms."

She shied, as he knew she would. Her color paled. "I shouldn't."

Joseph took her shoulders in his hands, stopping her retreat gently. "I will do nothing you are not comfortable with. You have my vow."

Berel looked around nervously, as if searching for people watching them.

"Do you trust me?" he asked.

She nodded, her blush returning.

"Then come to my rooms." Joseph took her hands, tugging gently to invite her forward.

Berel paused, meeting his eyes, then turned up the stairs. Joseph wrapped an arm around her waist, silently cheering her continued willingness. She entered his rooms calmly.

CHAPTER TEN

Joseph steered her past the bed. Berel wasn't ready for a move like that. He settled her on the wide lounging couch and placed a glass of the lizor berry wine she liked in her hand.

"Relax for a moment," he soothed her.

She drank a mouthful of the wine, sinking against the soft head of the couch. Joseph laid back next to her, toeing off his boots, his nerves humming in anticipation of the continuing lessons. Berel's eyes strayed from his, exploring the length of his body slowly. She took another drink of the wine as her gaze settled over his groin. His cock thickened in response to her perusal, and Berel locked on the sight, her hand tightening on the glass of wine.

Joseph took the glass, and she snapped her eyes to his face again. He sipped the sweet liquid, holding her gaze. He was too close to lose her to so ridiculous a thing. He leaned across her, teasing her with the barest touch of his body as he placed the wine on the low table beside her.

Berel laid a hand on his shoulder as Joseph crossed her body again. She licked her upper lip, and he was lost. Joseph kissed her, wrapping his hand around her hip and pulling her into the shelter of his body.

Her hands threaded through his hair and drew him closer, until Joseph was laid lightly over her. He guided the kiss to more fevered depths, allowing Berel to sink into her arousal in increasing increments.

Containing his mating instincts, as Berel ran her hands over his chest and through his hair, as she moved her body beneath his and pressed to him, was maddening. Joseph wanted to drive her further, but he was forced to let Berel become the aggressor and trust to the drive to mate of a mature Keen woman to push her on.

He ran his lips down her throat, nipping at the erogenous zone at her pulse point. Berel's scent intensified with the move, her female musk tantalizing Joseph's senses. It was the call to a mate, and resisting was impossible. He had to claim her soon.

Berel pulled up at his tunic, and he dragged it off for her. She stared at his chest, tracing her fingers over the curls and nipples, her eyes heavy, drunk on her own hormones more than the wine.

"Yes, Berel," he breathed. Joseph turned to his back, letting her drive take her.

She turned over him, continuing her exploration of his chest with shaking hands, her breath hot on his skin. Berel tasted him, rolling her tongue over a male nipple, making it painfully hard for her as she stole a bit of musk from him. She shivered in need, and he growled in frustration. Their mixed musk was quickly becoming an aphrodisiac mist around them.

Berel succumbed to the lure. She kissed him, beyond control, rubbing her hand over the bulge in his trousers. "So big," she breathed.

"For you."

She traced him, cupped him, gasped as he lengthened in her hand.

"Kiss me," he invited.

Berel didn't hesitate. She draped her body over his, moving restlessly, in need of his touch. Berel pulled his hand to her breast. "Touch me," she pleaded.

Joseph pulled the silin back from her breast. He suckled at her hard, at the limits of his control and knowing Berel needed a fierce touch in her mating frenzy.

She rolled her head, arching her back and pressing her core to him with whimpering cries. "Joseph, please."

"Tell me what you want," he ordered, moving his mouth to the opposite breast and grazing his teeth over the erect nipple.

"Touch me," she begged. "Touch all of me."

Joseph praised the design of the dress. It was an Earth style dress his mother had introduced to his sisters. The skirt was what Susan called 'a short wrap-around.' Joseph lifted Berel astride his body and separated the skirt to her waist, pulling it around her thighs. In effect, it was the Earth equivalent of a presentation dress.

Berel sought his hand as Joseph massaged her hood, drawing the moisture weeping from her slit to it as a lubricant. He bit back a groan as her skin warmed, the blood flow increasing as her body sought completion. The reaction forced more of her musk to her skin, speeding them toward a mindless frenzy. She had to demand more soon, or he'd disgrace himself and ruin his plan by climaxing outside her body.

There was only one way to urge her along the road he needed her to follow. Using the expertise he'd developed with eight years of schente, Joseph teased her body, using every erogenous zone to drive her to the edges of release but withholding that last touch that would send her over.

He knew the moment when he won his prize. Berel's eyes burned with a fierce inner light. She grasped the waistband of his trousers and tugged the buttons open, taking a ragged breath as she scanned her eyes over the length of his cock she'd uncovered.

"Do you want me?" he whispered, his control raw and his body aching.

She nodded.

"Take what you need."

Berel looked dazed, uncertain.

"Kiss me." He'd have to guide her.

She sank over him, moving her hips against him in a mute plea for his assistance. Joseph drew her hand to his cock and pressed her fingers to him, inviting her exploration. Berel stroked the corded veins, gasping as drops of his readiness welled up.

"For you," he invited.

Berel pulled his trousers down his legs, and Joseph kicked them away, impatient to consummate with her. She straddled his thighs, learning the contours of his body, her touch alternately soft and questing then hard and demanding. He panted back release.

"So hard," she breathed.

"For you. What do you want, Berel? Do you ache like I do?" He knew she did. The throbbing and heaviness of her sex had to be near maddening.

She closed her eyes, groaning, her scent a heady drug.

"Ease the ache. Take what we both need."

Berel rose up over him, guiding Joseph to her core. He placed his hands on her hips as she sank over him, fingerwidth by fingerwidth filling her engorged body.

Joseph stilled her as he felt her barrier, rejoicing that she hadn't had any experience at all with men. He was her first, and he would be her last if he had any say about it. "Stop. Let me take you over first," he offered. With his cock teasing at her barrier and his fingertips playing at her hood, he could make her shatter and take her to full completion on that high.

"Take it."

"Berel, it will hurt less."

She pushed down hard, screaming his name as the barrier tore. Joseph cried out with her, pulling Berel fully around him, feeling her barrier shatter to his thrust. Her eyes widened. Joseph started to soothe her, then sank into waves of delight as her sheath gripped him tight, pulsing around his length.

Berel gripped his shoulders, moving his length in and out frantically. Her body craved final completion. This was the moment Joseph had waited for.

"Do you want all of me?" he growled. She had to say it. The ceremony required that she ask for him.

"Joseph, please." Her movements were fevered.

He fought back climax. It had to be now. It had to be this first time that she asked him to go to completion in her. "All of me, Berel. My seed in you. My cock locked in your stim band. Is that what you want from me?"

"Yes. Finish it. Please." Her lips trembled, and her eyes closed on a sigh.

Joseph roared in triumph. He pushed deep inside her, filling her, his cock locking Berel to him and making them one. She howled out a formless scream as he swelled within her, her body stimulated to release an egg for him.

"That's right," Joseph breathed as she collapsed to his chest. He stroked his hands over her shoulders and back, drinking in her body's second climax.

Berel hadn't fainted as many maidens did when introduced to all three of the pleasures of a first mating in quick succession, as he'd heard Jenneane had with Tirin.

Still, she shivered, a look of stunned disbelief on her face. Joseph caressed her cheek, murmuring soothing words to her. He had known this would confuse her. He had been prepared for that.

He lessened. When his cock released her stim band, Joseph carried her to his bed and settled Berel beneath the silin sheets and a heavy quilt. He plucked a Cimmeg implin cake from the tray beside the table, already drizzled with heated sucre sap, and raised it to her lips. "Eat," he crooned. "The implin cake and sucre sap will restore your energy and the Cimmeg—"

"Will strengthen," she finished for him, smiling weakly. "I *am* a woman healer." She took a dainty bite of the sweet.

"I know. That's why I thought a Cimmeg scent was perfect for you." Joseph turned the lovers' repast and took a bite from the same spot she had, according to tradition.

Berel watched the move, her face draining of color. Her eyes shot from the tray of lovers' repast to the lizor berry wine to the length of his blood-stained cock to his face. "You planned this?" she asked, her breathing ragged.

Joseph returned the cake to her lips, waiting for her to take another bite before he started speaking. "I hoped you'd allow me to touch you. I prayed you would." He took his next bite, again encasing the print of her teeth on the cake.

She shook her head. "You wanted—"

He slid beneath the sheets, positioning himself over her, pressing his thickening member to her thigh. "I still want," he assured her.

Berel wasn't a woman to tumble and leave. He'd waited too long to let her walk away now.

"But—But, you're my—"

Joseph kissed her, tossing the cake at the tray and numbly noting that it bounced away from its target. Berel met him passionately, the fever of her mating frenzy still in full sway. She wrapped her leg around his thigh, seeking his cock blindly. Joseph cupped her buttocks in his hands and slid to the hilt in her.

Berel cried out, her eyes wide and unfocused. "Joseph," she gasped, though whether her plea was for him to stop or not to was left unsaid, perhaps not even clear to herself.

"I am not your brother," he assured her, punctuating his words with a sensuous stroke within her. "I don't want to be your brother." Another stroke. He stilled, lodged hard against her, as if at climax. "Is that really what you want? A brother?"

She shook her head frantically. Joseph smiled as he took her hard and fast. Despite Berel's earlier protests, she wanted the same thing he did. There was no question of that. Admitting it was simply hard for her.

Joseph groaned as he stimulated her band again. "Don't leave me, Berel. Promise you'll stay."

She nodded in exhaustion, her cheek pressed to his chest.

"Then by the right of Trial Moon, you won't leave," he crooned.

Berel mumbled something incoherent and fell asleep, still joined with him.

Joseph chuckled. "You won't remember that I said that. The morning will be a battle."

CHAPTER ELEVEN

Endl 13th, Ri 25-3010

Berel yawned deeply, snuggling under the quilt. Her muscles ached, and she made a mental note to make a lizor berry tea with olum, take a hot bath, and spend a lazy day in bed with a book. She slid from the bed, wondering at the fact that she'd slept in her clothing, and headed for the bath.

She hit her knee on the edge of a piece of furniture and recoiled, uttering a curse on Len as she rubbed the painful spot. Berel opened her eyes a slit, looking at the desk she'd hit in confusion, stilling with her hands wrapped around her sore knee. She glanced around the room, breathless, memories of the night before flooding her mind. Berel turned back to the bed, breathing a sigh of relief that Joseph wasn't there even as her heart foolishly ached that he wasn't.

"Oh no," she breathed, pressing a hand to her abdomen. She'd taken him completely unprotected. "Twice." Berel was a woman healer. How could she do something so utterly stupid?

Well, that was obvious. She wanted Joseph. She'd wanted him for years, but he had to make a contract his people would approve of.

A king cannot rule without the support of the nobles. Joseph had been taught that. Berel had heard it from Jole's mouth herself. Corin had taunted Berel with the truth of it, with the fact that Berel was not a match the nobles would support. As much as she would love to be the contract Joseph chose, she was lowborn, unacceptable to those Joseph needed to appease in order to rule.

She straightened her bodice and smoothed her skirt, pulling on the boots she'd pushed off at the couch. Her face heated at the scent of their sex on the rich, red fabric. It was too late to undo last night, but she wouldn't make a worse mistake. No promises had been made. Joseph could still fulfill his duty.

And if I conceive? Berel stifled a sob at that. She'd have the baby, of course. The law wouldn't stand for termination on one of the precious re-breds, and Berel couldn't bear the thought of killing a child Joseph had given her.

She'd raise the baby in a manner Joseph would approve of and let him have some say over that. Contract or no contract, Berel would have to let him be a part of their child's life. The longing might well kill her, but she wouldn't stand in the way of Joseph's duty, even if that meant seeing him with his chosen and their children when he came to see hers. He would be the next king of Kegin, no matter what it meant.

Resolved, Berel marched to the door and pulled it open, her back straight and chin high. Her breath caught at the sight of Joseph, a tray balanced on his arm and his free hand reaching for the door handle. His smile widened, making her heart stutter, and his bare chest was too close for her piece of mind. Her mouth watered at the memory of his taste.

"Hungry?" he asked, as if reading her longing to taste him again.

"I— No. I should go." She started to edge around him.

Joseph raised an eyebrow in disbelief. "We have to talk."

"That's not really necessary."

His eyes narrowed. "I took you without protection."

She winced. "I wasn't thinking clearly, and neither were you. If anything— We'll discuss it then." Again, she moved to pass his broad shoulders.

Joseph blocked her. "Sit down, Berel."

She backed off a step in shock. Joseph was ordering her. He hadn't done that since he was a boy of twelve.

His expression softened. "Sit down. Please."

Berel looked around in dismay. Sit down? Either the couch or the bed was a truly disconcerting option.

Joseph sighed. "Would you be more comfortable in my office?" he offered.

She nodded. *Anywhere but his bedroom.*

He stood back from the doorway and motioned to the door across the hall, as if she didn't know where his office was located. Berel took a calming breath and preceded him into the smaller room. She took a seat in front of his desk.

Joseph set the tray on the desk, well within her reach, and sat behind his desk, as if gleaning that she needed the space from him. "I don't want you to leave," he informed her calmly.

"Joseph, we can't do this," she reasoned.

"Why not? And don't start in about me being your brother again. We ended *that* discussion last night." His mouth quirked up in a half-smile.

Berel felt her face heat. Joseph had his proof of that. She'd admitted that she didn't want him as a brother. Her body had all but screamed the fact for him. She winced. She *had* screamed for him—several times.

"Why can't we pursue this?" he continued. "We're both adults." He steepled his fingers in front of his face.

"You have a duty."

Joseph smiled. "You're right. I do have a duty." He favored her with a hungry look that announced which portion of his duty he intended to perform again.

"Stop that." Pure self-preservation demanded that she snap him out of this somehow. "You're supposed to contract with a noblewoman and—" Her stomach rebelled at the thought of Joseph bedding one of the hopefuls who chased him.

He shook his head. "I was promised any willing woman on Kegin."

"Any willing woman?" Her head spun at his announcement.

"Contract with me."

Berel pushed back the spike of happiness. She'd done it. She'd caught his eye, but it wasn't enough. "Your father promised you, you mean," she stated miserably.

Joseph furrowed his brow. "I don't understand. Of course, my father did. And the Breeding Office," he added, as if that made a difference.

She bit back a sob. Joseph really thought that was enough. He probably believed Michael set a precedent by marrying the disavowed daughter of a general, a woman who was lowborn in the eyes of the nobles. *Well*— He had, in his own way. The nobility accepted his choice, because Michael had abdicated his right to the throne when he contracted. Danellan would never be queen.

"Contract with me," he offered.

"No." *He has a duty.* "I'm not willing."

Joseph shot her a look of disbelief. "You were certainly willing last night."

"I never promised a contract," she reminded him patiently. "It was—"

"What? Biology? Even the schen can't force a woman to a man she doesn't already want," he reminded her.

Berel forced her breathing to even. "A mistake," she whispered. *My mistake.* "We were drinking and in a mating frenzy."

His jaw tightened in fury. "I could prove you wrong. We're not drinking now. If I kissed you, you'd get wet for me again. Wouldn't you?"

She pressed a hand to her stomach. How could she argue that point when his voice alone had her prepared for him? When the thought of his body claiming hers again made her ache for him? Joseph scanned his eyes down her body, smiling as her nipples tightened for him, proving his point.

Berel pushed to her feet and stormed to the door. "I won't deny that I want you, but I won't contract with you." She shook her head. "I'm sorry, Joseph. I just can't."

"Sit down, Berel." He seemed exasperated with her.

"There's nothing more to say." *Except the one thing he could say that would crush me. How will I find the strength to walk away then?*

"You came to me willingly and took all I had to give. I'm not letting you go. Ever." His eyes burned in challenge.

She looked at him in dismay, gauging his resolve and finding Joseph immovable. Berel bolted through the door and down the corridor toward the rooms in the opposite wing. Jenneane would reason with him. Joseph's twin was her only hope.

Berel pounded on the door to Jenneane's rooms, gasping for breath and praying she and Tirin hadn't gotten an early start to their day.

"What is it?" Tirin grumbled, pulling the door open.

She locked on his half erect length, noting that Jenneane's mate had come directly from bed without pulling on a robe or lounging pants. For twenty years, she hadn't seen a naked man outside of a healing that couldn't wait for a proper doctor, and now she couldn't seem to escape the sight of unclothed men. Tirin's state of semi-arousal was the last thing her frazzled nerves needed.

Berel dragged her gaze to his face, suddenly remembering her purpose. "I need Jenneane. Please, Tirin." She squawked in protest as Joseph lifted her over his bare shoulder.

"Sorry we disturbed you, Tirin," he offered graciously.

"Jenneane," she screamed. "Call off your brother."

"Stay in bed, Jenneane," Joseph countered smoothly but with a hint of irritation in his voice. He turned as if to carry her back to his bed.

Berel reached for Tirin, catching the edge of the doorframe instead. "He's insane, Jenneane. You have to talk to him."

"What in Len's Dungeons is going on out here?" Jole demanded.

She raised her face fearfully. Jole Ri stood with his arms crossed over his bare chest and violence written on his features. Berel sent up a prayer of thanks to Fion that the man was at least wearing lounging pants. Susan surged into the corridor, belting a silin robe around herself. Other doors opened, and her adopted sibs peered at them in a mixture of curiosity and concern. Berel groaned.

"Just a misunderstanding, Father," Joseph offered brightly. "Sorry we disturbed you."

"If you don't mind," Berel snapped. "The blood is rushing to my head."

"Are you ready to talk to me?"

"Put me down, Joseph." Enough of his orders. Berel intended to issue a few of her own, starting with that one.

"Are you going to talk to me?" he demanded with less patience than the last time.

"Put her down," Jole ordered.

Joseph set her carefully on her feet, steadying Berel when her balance seemed uncertain.

She pushed his hands away. "Thank you, Jole. Now if you'll excuse me—" She started away.

Joseph snatched her wrist and pulled Berel back to his body, supporting her with a hand around her waist when she stumbled chest to chest with him. "Not so fast. We still have a conversation to finish."

Berel pulled at his hold. "We've finished," she informed him.

"Not remotely."

"Joseph," his father warned.

"There is more to this than you know," Joseph assured him.

"Then explain it quickly—please."

"Fine. I've declared my right to regit lus...*Trial Moon*." He used the ancient tongue then added the English translation, but why she couldn't guess.

Berel stilled, seeking out his face in outright fear. Joseph's determination left nothing to chance that she might have misheard him. "You can't."

"I have. You can't deny that I have the right." His smile was tight and strained. "Can you?"

She replayed the night before, fervently praying for anything she could use to argue the point. She groaned.

"I have the right," he attested.

"The practice doesn't exist," she countered hotly. "Not for the nobility. Not for centuries." It was true. No one but a lowborn had used Trial Moon in almost a millennium.

"It hasn't been banned. It simply hasn't been used because of the forced breeding measures."

Berel met Jole's eyes with a weak grin. "Would lodging a formal protest mean anything at all in this case?"

The king ran a hand through his hair,

considering the matter. "Of course it would."

Berel sighed in relief.

"It means I'll have to read the laws on this matter," he continued.

Joseph chuckled. "I've already done that," he noted.

Berel elbowed him in the stomach, letting her frustration take hold.

CHAPTER TWELVE

Joseph scowled at the group of women across the room. Berel was wrapped beneath Jenneane's arm, and his mother was just leaving the gathering to take her usual place beside Jole. Jenneane had all but vaulted from her bed when she'd heard about the Trial Moon. It was a miracle that Susan had somehow forbidden Eve and Rebecca to attend this meeting. At least that meant he only had to face down three rather upset women.

He grimaced at that. Joseph hadn't expected Berel to be so distraught over the idea of a Trial Moon. He'd thought she would balk for a few moments then resign herself to the month with him. He certainly hadn't expected her to lodge a formal complaint about it. Not after the night before. Not after she'd shattered over and over again in his arms.

The door opened, and Joseph turned to it. He felt his face heat as Syl shot him a hard look. Joseph felt three years old again, only this time he wasn't caught with a pocketful of stolen Gelgrin. This time he was caught making love to the woman healer's daughter and forcing her to a Trial Moon Berel *said* she didn't want.

Syl nodded curtly and crossed the room to her daughter. Berel dropped her gaze, her color darkening as Syl spoke to her in low tones.

Joseph muttered several harsh curses that only his father could hear. Berel felt shamed by this whole thing. For one mad moment, he considered withdrawing his demand. It wasn't too late for that. Since the issue was under protest, his father would happily accept his decision not to force this on Berel.

He swallowed a lump of frustration at the truth of the matter. It was too late to withdraw. Though his father would gladly release them, Joseph couldn't end it now. If he did, Berel would never give him another chance.

Jole cleared his throat, calling the proceedings to order. "I assume the provisions were met?" he asked delicately.

Joseph sighed. "Berel admitted that upstairs," he reminded his father.

She shot him a pained look. "I wasn't in my right mind."

"Did I do anything beyond kissing you without you requesting it? Did I do anything you didn't want me to do?"

Berel grimaced. "No. You know you didn't."

Joseph nodded grimly.

Jole shook his head. "The only irregularity is that the ceremony was traditionally held at the spring celebration...for the nobles, at any rate."

Berel took a calming breath. "Then it's not legal," she decided.

Joseph shook his head. "The only reason it happened then was because the parties at the celebration of Fion often got a little out of hand. Besides that, Berel wasn't legally an adult at the spring festival."

Jenneane offered an innocent-looking smile, leaving Joseph to wonder yet again if she was angry with him for this move or not. "You could have waited for the next spring festival," she suggested.

"That's not funny. You know how long I've been waiting for Berel. Another year would have killed me."

Berel rubbed her forehead as if she had a headache, and Joseph's cock stirred. If she were pregnant— No. It was too early for that. No baby implanted that fast.

She looked at Jole hopefully. "Is it legal or not?"

Jole considered the knot of women, Joseph, and finally Susan. If he'd hoped his bride would give him some indication of which way he should rule, he was in for a disappointment. Susan sat in her designated chair, her eyebrow raised and a slight smile on her face.

"This is a difficult decision. Berel is not happy about this arrangement, but I imagine not all the women who went to Trial were. The forms have been met, besides the traditional period of Trial royals have used. Joseph was promised any willing woman on Kegin, and Berel's actions reflect a level of...willingness."

Susan's smile widened at his tactful handling. "What will you do?"

"Compromise. The period of Trial typically ends at the end of this month. Joseph will have those twenty-four days rather than the full thirty-seven. The rules of Trial will be enforced. Joseph is bound. If Berel conceives or if she requests at any time, he will contract. If the month ends without a child between them or Berel's willingness, Joseph has no legal hold on her."

Joseph bit back a smile. Twenty-four days was better than a decision against him. He sobered, as Berel paled. Convincing her wouldn't be an easy task. If she didn't conceive in the next three weeks, she could leave him.

* * * *

"Eat, Berel. You're only going to make yourself ill."

She grimaced, pushing her food around the plate he'd set on the couch-side table. How could he expect her to eat when she felt like a prisoner? "Why did you do this?" She asked the question that had burned at her all morning.

"I meant what I said. I've been waiting for you. Not touching you over the last few years has been maddening."

"Why me? I never gave you any indication—"

Joseph laughed harshly. "You're unschooled in what you're doing, but you gave me indications." He leaned toward her, crowding Berel. "Do you know when you first did? When you gave me a sign that I knew I could not be mistaking? I can tell you, if you wish."

She shook her head, not willing to hear how clearly he'd read her longing. Joseph misunderstood her refusal—or pretended to.

"When you were seventeen, you came to *Christmas* celebration."

Berel nodded. She went to all the celebrations then, until shortly after Joseph and Jenneane

131

were of age.

"I danced with you."

She swallowed hard, remembering that dance all too well, Joseph holding her to his chest as they moved, his cock responding to her, pressing to her through her dress.

"Yes. You looked at me just like that." His voice dropped to a husky growl, and he traced her lower lip with one fingertip. "I wanted you that night, much more powerfully than I'd wanted you before it, and I've wanted you every night since."

Berel sank back to the raised head of the couch, her breathing ragged. "The Trial stipulations..." she whispered, unsure of whether she was asking him to convince her or stating her unwillingness.

Joseph turned halfway over her, stripping off his silin lounging pants and spreading her skirt as he had the night before. "You give yourself to me willingly?" he asked, his voice formal yet thick in arousal.

She nodded. The stipulations said she had to go to Joseph willingly but that he could entice her gently to willingness. As far as Berel could tell, he wouldn't have to entice her often. She was willing too often for her own comfort.

He smiled, a crooked lifting of his lips, and lowered his face, moving to the lower edge of the couch.

Berel stiffened. "What are you doing?"

Joseph lifted her leg around his body, spreading her wide. She shivered as he played the tip of his tongue inside her seam.

"You're a woman healer, Berel. You know what

I'm doing."

Driving me mad.

She shook her head, pleading silently for mercy as he drove his tongue deep. Joseph groaned, the sound rumbling through her womb. She cried out as he prodded her inner pleasure spot. His tongue retreated, replaced by two fingers. He played at her pleasure spot expertly.

"I can taste myself in you," he breathed. "Do you know how arousing that is?"

Her mouth went dry. "Taste?"

Joseph licked a torturous path around then over her hood. "They say the musk is ten times the aphrodisiac when taken internally."

She nodded. She'd read that, and it was part of her instruction as a woman healer. "Do you want me to taste you?" she asked, trying to follow his logic.

"When you're ready to." He licked at her hood again.

Berel gasped. "Would you find it as enjoyable as I find this?"

He buried his tongue in her again, and she bowed up. Joseph pressed the pad of his thumb to her hood, playing his tongue over the pleasure spot. She shattered around him, jerking as he cried out with her.

Joseph climbed up beside her, trembling as he gathered her into his arms. "That is how good it would feel," he managed in a thick voice, drunk on her fluids, needing more from her though he was obviously denying himself.

Berel raised her head, licking a line through the slick on his chin. The flavor was a mix of sweet spice and tangy musk. She groaned, sucking more in. The throbbing was more insistent now. Joseph hadn't taken her to full completion.

And you're complaining? You can't have a child if he doesn't stimulate you.

She was complaining! Her body was adamant. Joseph would finish what he started.

Joseph pulled her hard to his erection as she cleaned the last of their mixed juices from his face. "In my bed," he growled.

Berel nodded shakily. "Yes."

"Without that dress."

She reached for the tie at the waist, but Joseph's hands were there first. He barely breathed as he unfastened the hook and drew it over her shoulders and down her arms.

Joseph gazed at her, his eyes moving up and down slowly to take in all of her. "I've wanted to do this forever." He scooped his arms under her knees and back, rising from the couch with her cradled to his chest, leaving her dress behind.

He followed Berel down onto his bed, taking the peak of one nipple into the heat of his mouth. She arched against him, awash in the new sensations of his body against hers.

The thick mat of curls on his chest tantalized her abdomen, waking her body to half-remembered delights of the previous night. She gasped, her internal muscles throbbing in need of the thrusts of his body.

Joseph's mouth trailed to the opposite nipple. His movements were slow, tender, not at all what she wanted of him. She wanted the wild joining she remembered so well, Joseph piercing her body and informing her that he was not her brother.

Berel gripped his hair and guided his mouth to hers, letting her impassioned kiss voice her plea for him. Joseph didn't question her intent. His cock filled her in a single thrust, an exquisite counterpoint to her body's throbbing. He smiled as if her body told him a delightful secret. She wrapped her legs around his hips, urging him on in words and action. His thrusts were fierce, fast, everything she wanted of him.

She'd barely recognized the first mind-altering waves of her climax when the heat of his seed stole her breath. Then he was locked in her, his hips pressed tight to hers, her body exploding in sensation. The shocks of her egg releasing were eclipsed by the heat washing through her womb and riding her nerve pathways to all of her body, the continuing spasms of her climax, Joseph's hair teasing her flesh, his mouth on hers, stealing her scream with a kiss that made her ache for more of him.

Joseph pulled back slightly, breaking off the kiss. His voice was low and gruff, almost an order. Her fevered mind translated his English for her.

I love you, Berel. I will accept no one else. Do not deny me this. It has always been you.

It was so tempting to take him to her heart, but one of them had to be realistic. No Keen ruler had ever married a servant. If Joseph contracted with her, he might as well abdicate and waste all those years of training as heir apparent. If he knew that giving up his future for her was the price, would he still be so intent?

Regardless, she couldn't allow it. Joseph had been raised to his place, as Berel had been raised to hers. He would make a good king, perhaps a better king than Jole made. None of the others in line would serve nearly as well.

CHAPTER THIRTEEN

Endl 19th, Ri 25-3010

Joseph did his best to mask his frustration as Berel dressed in one of the silin gowns he'd had stored in his cabinet for her. When she'd turned to him so readily after his father's decree, Joseph had believed the fight was all but over. It wasn't.

Berel's invitation had wilted for reasons unknown. She shied from his touch, and though she shared his bed, Berel was as distant as she'd be if she inhabited her own quarters. For six days, he'd been tortured by her refusal.

He had no idea why Berel refused him. When he'd asked, she'd simply said that their union wasn't meant to be. Joseph had no clue what Berel could mean. They were sexually compatible, and she was emotionally affected by him. In addition, they knew each other well. What could be missing?

She headed for the door, her eyes down, fiddling with her woman healer's bracelet. Joseph reached out and took her hand, shaking his head.

"What is it?" Her voice shook lightly.

"Spend the day with me."

Berel looked toward the door, hiding her face from him, most likely concocting a reason to refuse. "I should—"

"You checked on Jenneane yesterday." *Though she wasn't due for an examination for almost a month, and she certainly isn't in distress, despite*

137

the fact that she conceived again so quickly. "You checked on your supplies the day before." *And took all day for a task I know from experience is an hour or so of work.* "You—"

She spoke over him. "I should—"

"Spend the day with me." Joseph stroked her hand, praying she'd bow to this request.

She nodded slowly. "As you wish."

Joseph sighed, sending up a fervent prayer that Berel wanted to spend the day with him, no matter how much she protested outwardly. "Good. First we will see to breakfast."

He led her out the door, turning her toward the main stairs when she veered toward the far corner of the palace and the servants' stairs. He pretended not to see her backward glance or the crimson tint of her cheeks. He guided her to the dining room. Thus far, Berel had neatly avoided eating anywhere but their room or the kitchen. That was the first thing Joseph intended to change.

The dining room was all but deserted. Most of the family had eaten and turned to their duties or diversions already. Only Neane, Tirin, and their son remained.

"Good morning, Berel," Neane called brightly.

Berel managed a tight smile in reply, and Neane's smile faltered. His sister met Joseph's gaze with a pained look as Berel took a seat at the table. Thankfully, she sat to the right of the chair Joseph usually used, saving him the trouble of moving down to sit next to her.

Joseph guided her chair to the table and settled in his own, nodding his thanks to the servants who set plates before them.

"So what are your plans today?" Neane asked.

"If you need me," Berel began, a touch of desperation in her voice.

"She doesn't," Joseph interrupted. "You promised me the day. If something does come up, I'm sure your mother can handle it."

Berel nodded, picking at her food.

Tirin glanced from Berel to Joseph, his expression giving the impression that he was considering something as grave as battle strategy. "Don't you have a meeting with Ambassador Lian today?" he asked.

Joseph groaned. He'd forgotten his meeting with the Keen Ambassador to Wolkin. It was an important meeting, one Joseph had prepared for weeks to tackle.

"If it's a bad day," Berel suggested.

"No," he replied. "The meeting is in an hour, and it won't last long. Come with me."

She shot Neane a pleading look, as if she hoped his twin would come up with an excuse for her to refuse. Seeing no such aid forthcoming, Berel nodded. "Of course."

* * * *

Berel glanced at the papers strewn across Joseph's desk. There were notes scribbled in his neat handwriting about trade routes and cargo, temporary personal visits, and landing sites near markets for Wolkin wares. Joseph was bent to work on one of these. His dedication to making the agreement work was apparent in his single-minded attention.

She watched him, transfixed on his pen moving, the blue ink he loved so dearly in stark contrast to the black and white of the printed page. As if entranced, Berel found herself stroking the choc waves of his hair.

His pen stilled, and he turned to her, his eyes questioning. Berel looked at the hand buried in his hair in dismay and started to pull away.

Joseph's hands closed around her waist and lifted Berel to his desk, her bottom planted firmly on the notes for his meeting. "Don't leave," he whispered.

That simply, Berel had no drive to leave him. Joseph's blue eyes were dark as a stormy sea, pleading for her compliance. He held her gaze, his hand skating over her knee and up her thigh to the erogenous zone at her pulse point. Joseph stroked it gently.

Berel sucked in her breath in surprise, her body dampening for him. He stroked again—and again, coaxing a response from her.

"Open for me." It wasn't a request. Joseph spoke calmly, an order from a man accustomed to being obeyed.

She spread her legs wide without question, planting her feet on the arms of his chair and leaning back on her elbows, open to him.

Joseph ran his thumbs up the line of her pulse, stroking lightly. His fingers settled at the join of her thighs and buttocks, tracing the seam. Berel threw her head back as her body responded, knowing what would happen next. His thumbs caressed the line of her hips. He started the path again, making her ache for more.

"Bel tro," she gasped. Mother Fion, where had Joseph learned to perform the bel tro?

Joseph's lips touched one pulse point and then the other, his hands tracing the ancient path, over and over.

Berel jerked as he eased her toward the edge of the desk, knowing his next move would shatter her. The bel tro was legendary. The man who could perform it correctly was rare. It must have taken Joseph years to perfect it.

He was suddenly standing between her thighs. Berel met his eyes in mute surrender. Joseph rocked his hips along her sensitized thighs, his hands closing around her waist. He kept eye contact, rocking closer so that his cock slid back and forth between her outer slit.

"Berel?" Joseph's voice was low, questioning her agreement.

She started to nod, needing him to finish the ancient rite. According to the texts Berel had read, possession taken in the bel tro would be unlike anything she would otherwise experience, more intense than any other sexual encounter in existence.

A brisk knock sounded.

Joseph cursed fluently. "Wait," he barked.

Berel shook her head, easing away from him. "No," she whispered. "Your duty."

"I'm doing my duty," he grumbled.

She blushed. "We can't— Not now."

He nodded. "Later. Promise me. Give me your vow."

She hesitated. What would he do if she refused? Joseph's true duty was this meeting. If agreeing would make him attend to it... "Yes," she assured him. "Yes. You have my word." She glanced at the door, trying to straighten her dress. "Now, please. Please, see the ambassador."

Joseph nodded.

Berel slid to the floor, squatting to grasp a paper that she'd pulled off with her and tossing it to the desk. She reached for his trousers, her mind spinning. Would the ambassador be able to tell what he'd interrupted?

He sat, pulling away from her ministrations, then lifted her onto his lap, scooping her legs over the arm of his chair. His cock pressed into the curve of her buttocks, a clear reminder of what she'd agreed to.

"Joseph, you can't," she gasped.

"I can and I will."

* * * *

Joseph smiled at Berel's look of stunned disbelief. Why shouldn't he do this? Ambassador Lian wouldn't be able to see his state of undress, and his trousers would be more than painfully tight if he closed them. He guided Berel's face to the base of his throat, putting the last of his plan in motion.

Let the ambassador think what he liked. After seeing the stark need in Berel's eyes, Joseph wasn't letting her out of his arms anytime soon. She was aroused, and the combination of his musk and the feeling of his ready length would keep her that way.

"Come in," he ordered.

The door opened, and Lian entered the room. The man stopped, scanning his eyes over Berel in stark male interest. Joseph cleared his throat, giving the ambassador a look of warning. Lian dropped his gaze in understanding, sinking to the chair provided for him.

Berel's breath was hot on his skin, slight tremors passing through her form.

"The Wolkin," Joseph began, trying to ignore his body's insistent straining toward her. "This agreement has been debated since my great grandfather's day."

"With no success until now," Lian noted. "You and your father have brought the fine art of diplomacy to the discussions."

Joseph smiled. "My thanks, Lian. Now, if you will take the file before you, I have set out your limitations, the agreement we'd like to get and the minimum we will accept. I trust your negotiation skills."

Lian bowed his head in thanks then buried himself in the file Joseph had compiled for him.

Joseph took the opportunity to glance at Berel. He stroked her hip slowly beneath the desk, smiling as her breathing hitched. He closed his eyes, picturing Berel as she lay across his desk, her eyes slumberous and her body open to him, under the spell of the bel tro.

It had taken Joseph almost three years to master the rite. Millennia before Ro Ti unified Kegin under his rule, a Magden King could not take his place unless he subdued his bride with the bel tro. While he had used his schente to practice, it had always been Berel he'd pictured under his hands.

He traced her hip again then stroked the cleft where her thigh and buttocks met. Berel's breathing quickened. Her body, sensitized by the bel tro, reacted to each touch as if he followed the full circuit. Her nipples stood out against the silin gown.

"This percentage is very generous. You are willing to go that low?" Lian asked.

Joseph took a deep breath, inhaling Berel's rising scent. He forced his mind back to the subject at hand. "Only if all of our major concerns are met in regard to landing sites, rules for visiting aliens, and cargo limitations."

He ran his fingertips up her inner thigh, stopping as she wiggled against him, scattering his senses. The feeling of the silin and her warmth brushing over the engorged tip of his cock was nearly too much for him.

"I don't think the cargo restrictions and landing sites will cause problems, but they may request changes to the regulations for visitation." Lian's voice seemed to come from far away.

Joseph didn't look at him. "Why would they be unacceptable?" he inquired. His tongue felt thick and unresponsive.

Berel's lips pressed to the pulse point on his neck. Her breasts jutted forward as she inhaled his scent.

"It revolves around a religious observance...of some sort. I've told you how secretive they are about their culture."

"Yes. You have." The words were filtering into his muddled mind but not making much of an impression along the way as they ordinarily would.

"While they go about their daily lives, they do not travel three days of every month. If they come here just before that cycle, they will request permission to stay until it ends."

Joseph nodded, brushing his chin through Berel's hair. "Provisionally," he decided. "As long as there are no problems, they may have the time to meet their religious obligations."

Berel's hand slipped between their bodies, circling his cock and pulling it free to the space between them. She teased him, stroking the sweet spot beneath the head with her fingertips. He stiffened, forcing his breathing to even. She tipped her head back, watching him from beneath half-closed eyelids.

"Then I see no problems with finalizing the agreement," Lian decided.

Joseph didn't answer. He couldn't seem to form words. Berel's scent intensified.

"Your Highness?" Lian asked. "Prince Joseph?"

He snapped his attention to the ambassador, noting Lian's smile and his flaring nostrils as he drew in the rising scent of musk in the enclosed room. If his cock were not hidden by the file, Joseph felt certain he would see Lian rising in response to the aphrodisiac—and the diplomat was looking at Berel.

"Then we have nothing left to discuss," Joseph snapped, the need to remind Lian of his place making his voice more gruff than it would typically be.

Lian's eyes widened, and he looked away from Berel. "No, Highness. The negotiations should go smoothly."

"Then leave us."

He rose and strode out the door, his eyes studiously averted.

Joseph didn't even wait for the door to latch before he brought his mouth down on Berel's. Lian no doubt knew his intent; and Keen, especially re-bred Keen, were hardly known for their patience in sexual matters. She shifted on his lap, giving herself the room to stroke him more purposefully.

"My bed," he rasped, moving from her mouth to the well of musk at her throat. "I want to complete the bel tro." He didn't intend to do that on his desk again.

She dropped her head back, opening her neck for his ravenous mouth. "Later," she whispered.

"Your word." He worked his way back up to her jaw then her mouth. Joseph had to have her vow that she'd let him complete the rite before he took her in some rash manner, as their bodies demanded. He moved his lips to her cheek, allowing her to answer, nearly groaning at her gasping breaths.

"You have it. Please, Joseph. I can't—"

Berel made it no further. Joseph laid her across his desk again, sending pens and papers skittering off the edge, wrapping his hands around her inner thighs and opening her to his first thrust. She moaned softly, arching her back to entice him deeper.

"Mine," he gasped, driving her on, taking her deeper, harder, groaning at her incoherent sounds of pleasure.

Her eyes opened wide as Joseph lodged deep inside of her, his cock erupting. Berel pressed down hard on him, her body beginning to contract as he locked into the stim band. They cried out together, Berel in the mixed sensations of her overlapping climaxes and Joseph in the knowledge the he was one step closer to a contract.

* * * *

Berel lingered in the bathroom, pressing a hand to the ache in her womb. Her body still vibrated in the glow of the bel tro, and the wild joining on Joseph's desk had only intensified her need.

It was dangerous to allow Joseph to resume the ceremony. Legend said that a woman who was taken in bel tro would crave her lover's touch, that she'd never wish to know the touch of another.

She chided herself as a fool. Berel had known with Joseph's first kiss that she'd never turn to another man, that she'd want more of him for as long as she lived. What would change with the addition of the bel tro?

"Nothing." But still she tarried. "Coward," she breathed.

"Berel," Joseph called, a clear indication that he knew she was procrastinating.

"In a moment," she answered, forcing her voice to even. Berel looked at her reflection, grimacing at the haunted look in her eyes. "Coward. Go out there and face him. Mag demands adherence to vows."

Berel spun on her heel and marched into the bedroom. She faltered, panning her gaze over Joseph.

He stood, leaning against one of the posts at the foot of his bed, gloriously naked. His tanned arms were crossed over his broad chest, his legs spread in battle stance, his cock hard and ready.

She pressed a hand to her womb again, cursing her arousal silently. All Joseph had to do was look at her, and she wanted him. When he spoke, she melted. She was his for the price of a single touch.

He spoke quietly. "Take off your robe." It wasn't an order. It was a lover's voice.

Berel's hands moved to the tie, letting it fall then easing the robe off her shoulders. Joseph's eyes didn't follow the movement of the silin as it pooled around her ankles. He kept his eyes locked on hers, drawing her into the depths of fathomless blue.

He didn't speak again. Joseph waited for her, knowing Berel would come to him, and come she did. She gasped in the realization that she was moving to him, gliding toward his body as if he held her entranced. She stopped before him, the heat of his body like the touch of silin over her skin. Berel waited, fully aware that her eyes pleaded with Joseph for his touch.

Joseph didn't speak. He didn't move. His eyes held hers. Berel pressed her body to his, seeking Joseph's mouth, desperate to make him act.

His kiss was slow and thorough. She reached for his hands, pulling them to her hips. Without the barrier of his crossed arms between them, Berel laid her body fully against his, his cock hot and heavy against her hipbone.

Berel gasped as his fingers traveled along the seam of her thigh and buttocks. She dropped her head back, offering her body to him.

"You still feel it," he whispered, stroking her hips.

Her legs shook.

"Tell me to stop."

Berel pulled her head up, training bleary eyes on his tense jaw and full lips, shaking her head in confusion.

"If I resume the bel tro, I won't stop until it's done."

She nodded.

Joseph stroked his fingertips along her lips. "You want this?"

"I—" She swallowed, trying to follow his logic without success. "I promised," she reminded him.

"No. I don't want your promise. I don't want your acceptance. I want you to want it. Do you?" He trailed his fingers down her jaw to her throat. "Do you want it?"

"Yes." She did. If Joseph didn't finish what he'd started, this ache would never end.

Berel expected him to smile at her admission. He didn't. He moved his hand to her inner thigh and watched her expression as he stimulated the lines and started the pattern again.

She grasped at his ribs, her legs' ability to hold her weight uncertain. "Joseph, I can't..."

Joseph nodded, scooping Berel into his arms and laying her on his bed, pulling her knees up and out. The bel tro began again, his hands tracing the pattern tirelessly.

Berel groaned as Joseph took full advantage of her arousal. His touch was everywhere. His mouth made slow, warming trails over her breasts, dipped into her navel, nipped at the source of her musk at pulse points all over her body.

"The texts don't mention this," she pleaded.

Joseph chuckled, his breath sending shocks not unlike completion over her sensitized skin. "You're right," he admitted. His lips pressed to the pulse points inside her thighs; then his thumbs returned.

She groaned, her entire body going boneless. Berel sank into waves of pleasure, the air hot in her lungs and her muscles weak. The expectation of Joseph's possession was maddening. "Joseph, please."

"You'll be ready soon," he promised.

"I am," she gasped.

"No. I rushed you earlier. When it's time, we'll both know."

The bel tro went on. Berel reached for him, but her hand slid from his shoulder. She shifted, cursing her inability to pull him over her, to invite him into her body. She groaned.

Joseph raised his head, meeting her eyes. Berel lost herself in pools of deep blue that seemed to undulate before her, slipping further under his spell with every heartbeat. She gasped at the sensation that their hearts were beating in unison. She moved her lips as if to speak, but her body betrayed her.

He moved forward, lifting Berel beneath her thighs, his hips following the path that started and ended the bel tro. Joseph didn't ask her permission this time. He didn't move his gaze from hers.

His cock breached her body, and their shared heartbeat sped. His hips rocked forward and back, keeping quarter meter perfection with the beat. Berel moaned, shivering as Joseph matched even that.

The pressure built, making Berel's body tingle, then burn. Her muscles tensed, and then it came—the moment when he became part of her, printed in her genes themselves.

She screamed, joined by Joseph, their sounds overlapping until even she couldn't tell which was which, pushed beyond endurance, the connection between them painfully sweet. His cock pulsed inside her, his heat eclipsing hers.

Joseph locked inside her, completing the sensation that they were one. Berel flattened a hand on his chest, a tear spilling down her cheek in the realization that his heart really did keep time with hers, that every breath they took was in unison. They *were* one being, eye to eye, body to body, heart to heart.

He planted his hands next to her head, lowering his body over Berel's carefully, capturing her lips in a slow, solemn kiss. His lips left hers and trailed over the tear. "I rushed you earlier."

"How did you..." Berel faltered, gasping with Joseph as he circled a thumb over one tight-drawn nipple.

His cock pulsed inside her, another jet of his heat invading her core. His voice was rough; arousal given a form, it caressed her mouth. "I practiced. Tirelessly."

"Schente?"

Joseph nodded, something she'd classify as fear in his eyes.

Berel fought back something beyond jealousy at the thought of him sharing this with a schente, something creating a painful band in the vicinity of her heart. It was too precious—this sharing of souls that came with the bel tro. She sobbed as his cock lessened and the connection faded with it, her heart stuttering then adopting a rhythm that set her apart from him again.

As if reading her thoughts, Joseph cupped her cheek in his hand, shaking his head, his eyes wide. "Never," he assured her. "I never took a schente to completion in the bel tro, Berel. It nearly killed me to stop, but the bel tro was for you. Only for you." His lips caressed hers. "I will never use it on another."

Berel tried to still the trembling of her lips with little success. "Then how could you know it would work?"

Joseph kissed her more fiercely, his hands exploring her body as if mapping what he owned. "I wouldn't fail you," he growled. "I will never fail you."

The question remained. Could she convince herself not to fail him?

CHAPTER FOURTEEN

Endl 20th, Ri 25-3010

Berel entered Joseph's office. Her smile fled as he turned to her and she met his eyes. His fury was impossible to miss. She backed off a step, abruptly uncertain.

"Berel," he greeted her without warmth.

"You called for me?"

Joseph motioned to his desk. "A message was delivered."

"For me?" she asked in confusion.

He nodded, a muscle twitching in his jaw, his eyes hard.

"You read it?" A niggling of anger gained force.

He nodded once, a tense snap of his head.

"How dare you. Being a prince gives you no right to read my—"

"It's a good thing I did," he growled.

"What is that supposed to mean?" she snapped.

Joseph scooped the missive up, marched to her, and pushed it into her hands.

"Perhaps someone should have taught you—" she began.

"Read it," he ordered.

Berel glared at him, trying to decipher how she'd missed this side of him for the last twenty years.

"Read it."

She dropped her gaze to the sheet in her

hand, taking in the details. Verda Laes had received Berel's missive. While the noblewoman was upset by the delay, she respected that the royal family had enticed Berel to remain for another month. For the prize of claiming a royal woman healer, the lady could afford to be gracious, and so she was. That was one of the many reasons Berel had decided to make her home with Verda.

Berel folded the missive, not meeting his eyes. "You had no right to read this," she informed him.

"You have nothing else to say to me?"

"What is there to say?"

"You intended to leave without saying a word, didn't you? Verda expected you a few days after your passage."

"Yes. She did."

Joseph's hands closed on her shoulders. "You would have walked away without a word to anyone. Jenneane wants you here for her child's birth. She expects that you will be."

Berel winced at that. If anything could hold her here a little longer, Jenneane would be that one person.

Liar!

"Why were you leaving?" he asked.

She shook her head, unwilling to admit how much he'd affected her, even when she'd had no hopes that he wanted her.

"You didn't tell Verda why you were delayed," he noted. "What will you do if—"

"You won't," she blurted out.

"You still intend to leave me. You're just biding your time until you're free to walk away." He didn't question it. He didn't have to.

Tears burned in her eyes. "*You* asked for the Trial Moon, Joseph. I could have been gone without putting either of us through this."

"Without..." Joseph cursed fluently in both Keen and English. "You are not unaffected. When I touch you—"

Berel closed her eyes, aching for him. "We are not meant to be," she whispered, pleading with herself as much as she was with him.

"We are," he insisted.

"No. You have your duty. You've been raised to be king, as I have been raised to be a woman healer."

"They aren't mutually exclusive."

"They are."

He raised his voice, frustration and the hint of an order projecting to her. "I don't see—"

She shook her head, shaking off his hands and turning to leave.

Joseph didn't attempt to hold her again, but he did speak in a voice that brought her to a halt at the door. "I'm not letting you leave me without a fight," he warned. "I will not allow you to dismiss me this simply."

Berel sighed, retreating to the safety of her storeroom. "Simple?" she grumbled. "He thinks *this* is simple?"

Nothing was simple. She had to avoid Joseph as much as possible. If possible, she had to convince him that this was a bad idea.

Most of all, Berel needed to research the history of the Trial Moon. She needed to know what the particulars of the laws were, what ancient royals had used it, and what the outcomes of those Trials were.

CHAPTER FIFTEEN

Endl 22ⁿᵈ, Ri 25-3010

Joseph startled at the knock on the door, forcing his eyes open to the darkness around him. "What is it?" he snapped.

"Many pardons." The male voice was tense but breathless, as if he'd run some considerable distance. "I seek Healer Berel. Her mother is in the village for a birth and—"

"Here," she replied.

The bed shifted as Berel fairly leapt to her feet. A light flicked on, and Joseph blinked his eyes, watching her dress in growing understanding. He pushed to his feet, reaching for the clothing he'd folded over the bedside table.

"What is your need?" Berel asked.

"My bride...Juberin—"

"I know," she assured him, pulling on her boots and reaching for her pack.

"What is it?" Joseph asked, dragging a tunic over his head to complete his dressing.

She turned to him, her eyes widening. "Joseph, you—"

"Does her husband possess the healing magic?" he asked pointedly, tucking the tunic into his trousers.

Berel blushed. "Of course not, but—"

"Then my help would be beneficial."

She nodded, though she seemed uncertain.

"It is my duty to help where I can," Joseph

reminded her.

"Of course." Berel rounded him and opened the door, offering the young soldier a strained smile. "Tralean," she greeted him.

"I have a mare..." He broke off, bowing his head to Joseph, his eyes wide. "My apologies, Highness. I did not know—"

"No need," Joseph assured him, pushing back his irritation at the vision of Tralean sharing a mount with Berel. He motioned to a roving soldier. "Noric and Tubri," he ordered, "before we reach the main hall."

The soldier took off at a run.

"Jenneane's buck?" Berel asked.

Joseph wrapped an arm around her waist and steered Berel toward the main stairs. "You know Tirin doesn't allow Jenneane to ride when she's carrying. She will thank you for exercising her mount." *And Tralean will have no need to touch you.*

No one spoke as they made their way down to the front doors.

As he'd ordered, the soldier was returning on Tubri's back, leading Noric behind. He slid to the ground and offered both sets of reins to Joseph. He took them with a nod, then took the pack from Berel's shoulder and lifted her to Tubri's back, smoothing her trouskit.

He mounted Noric smoothly, taking up his reins and offering Berel a wide smile. "We'll ride on, Tralean," he announced to the soldier accepting his mare from the same guard who'd brought their mounts to Joseph and Berel.

Berel led the way, guiding Tubri through the

side gate and over the foothills to the further barracks. She swung down at a common cabin and tethered Neane's mount to a grazing ring at the corner. Joseph did the same, noting Tralean topping the far hillside as he followed Berel inside.

Two women jumped to their feet as he entered, bowing deeply, seemingly terrified by his presence. Joseph waved them away, his gaze settling on the woman in the bed.

Juberin was coated in sweat, her hair hanging limp around a pale face. Her hands were placed over her womb, and her eyes were locked on Berel's, pleading silently for help.

Berel took her pack from Joseph, settling it on the foot of the bed. "Is the pain severe yet, Juberin?" she asked.

"Less," she panted.

"Less than the last two times?" Berel asked patiently.

Juberin nodded, her dark-ringed eyes closing. "It is early."

"What is it?" Joseph asked.

Berel motioned to one of the women at the table. "Bathe her head." She pulled the Auguren and Felgren soap from her pack and started washing her hands at the sink. Just when Joseph thought she'd ignore him, Berel spoke. "Juberin carries well, but her children do not survive birth—until now, I hope."

"Why?"

"Her body releases a surge of Oxykol when labor begins."

Joseph sucked in his breath in shock. He'd never heard of a toxic response like that before.

His mind spun. An injection of the antitoxin now would cause a shock that would kill at least the child and possibly the mother, as well. Without relief, the poison would do the same.

"My healing," he offered, stammering over his words. It was the only way.

"Would you?" Berel didn't look up when she asked, but her shoulders tensed slightly.

He turned to the young bride. "I offer my healing. I can reduce the toxin in your system naturally, slowly, the way it is meant to be done." Fion! Why had no one ever asked for his help before? How many children had this woman lost?

Tralean walked through the door, and Juberin looked to him, tears in her eyes, seemingly beyond speech.

"What is it?" he asked. "The babe?"

"His... The Pr..." Her lips trembled, and tears spilled down her cheeks.

"I've offered my healing," Joseph explained. "To reduce the toxins." He met Tralean's startled gaze. "With your leave to do so."

Tralean motioned to his bride, nodding frantically. "Anything to save them," he pleaded.

Berel returned to the bed. "Tralean, massage the nerve bundle in her lower back. Joseph, the healing."

No one spoke save whispered orders from Berel. There was too much work to do for useless chatter. Joseph forced toxins from Juberin's system that the women washed away with warm cloths, fetching clean water every quarter of an hour to accomplish the task. Tralean massaged her back, whispering encouragement to his bride.

Between the two, the laboring woman relaxed into the birth as she should have, free from pain at last.

"We will have our child," Tralean promised. "We were quick enough this time."

"All is well," Berel assured him. "Your child is moving against my hand."

Tralean sighed in relief. "You see? Our child will survive this time."

Joseph glanced at Berel, but she didn't spare him an answering look. She was beautiful in her concentration.

"Soon, Juberin," Berel soothed her.

"Yes," she agreed. "I feel it."

Joseph alternated between soothing the toxins in her system and watching the babe ease into Berel's hands. She acted quickly, freeing the babe from her mother's body, administering a hypocil of the antitoxin to the child and wrapping her in a tiny quilt as the babe started to cry.

Juberin sobbed into her husband's shoulder, seemingly oblivious to the hypocil of antitoxin Berel gave her, uttering thanks to the gods and to everyone in the room.

Berel tucked the hypocil back into her bag. "A precaution," she assured Joseph in a whisper. She picked up the wrapped babe again and stood. "Your daughter, Juberin," she offered brightly, though tears pooled on her eyelashes. "You may need to feed her now. The hypocil has awakened her."

Tralean helped her support their daughter to her breast. He met Joseph's eyes and offered his hand. "I am in your debt, Highness. Ask anything of me."

Joseph smiled, clasping his forearm. "No. It was my pleasure to serve. Call for me when your bride presents you with another child. It will be my honor to assist."

He nodded, swallowing hard.

Berel continued her work, giving instructions, seeing the new family settled, and packing up the last of her tools and herbs. Joseph swelled in pride that this woman was his—if he could bind her to him.

* * * *

Berel glanced at Joseph out of the corner of her eye, smiling at the ease with which he joined the revelry. Davira handed him a mug of iri brandy, and Joseph took it, laughing and raising it to the couple on the bed.

"May Fion bless you with many more, my friends," he offered.

"Zirhah," the cry went up.

"Zirhah," Berel cheered, drinking a mouthful of the brandy from her own mug.

"To Healer Berel," Tralean called. "Twice, you have saved my bride and cried over my lost sons, sharing our pain. Now, you rejoice in our gain. Know you are welcome at our table any time you wish to partake of a meal with us."

"Zirhah," the others shouted, Joseph the loudest of all. He caught her eye as he drank from his mug, radiating arousal.

Berel took a shaky swallow of her brandy. "It

was Joseph," she began.

"To Healer Berel," Juberin added, a mug of lizor berry tea in her hand. "I honor you. I give you my daughter, Berisa."

Berel gasped at the gift of a namesake. She'd never thought that someone would grant her such a thing.

"May Fion grant you many strong babies," Juberin continued.

Joseph drank deeply of his mug, the gleam in his blue eyes making her breathless in desire. Berel stared into her mug, torn. If she didn't drink, she'd offend Juberin. If she did, she'd encourage Joseph.

She met his gaze, remembering the bel tro. Even now, she could almost feel his heart beating, his body and soul one with hers. Berel drank deeply, the brandy burning a trail through her body and warming nerves already sensitized in her arousal.

The room had gone still and silent. Berel looked around in confusion, blushing at the knowing looks the soldiers and their wives sent Joseph and herself. Of course, word would have spread that Tralean had summoned her from Joseph's bed.

Berel cleared her throat, taking another drink of the brandy and blinking back tears at the fiery liquid. "I will inform the clinic that you'll arrive this morning," she instructed Juberin.

"I will send a transport for you," Joseph offered.

Tralean motioned to Captain Levsi. "The Captain," he began.

Joseph scowled. "A troop transport? Or a supply transport? No. Not this time. You are relieved from duty for the length of your bride's mother's fast. I will not permit any threat to this child," he vowed. He looked at Berisa, his expression softening. "You have lost too much."

Juberin recovered first. "Our thanks, Highness. We can never repay this kindness."

"There is nothing to repay," Joseph assured her. He turned to Berel, draining the last of his mug. "But it is time for us to be away."

Taking Joseph's hint, Davira rushed forward, placing Berel's pack in her hands and retreating with the mug. A titter of laughter warmed the room.

Berel turned to Joseph, wishing she'd drained her mug before allowing Davira to take it. Joseph put his hand out to her, and she went to him, letting him lead her out of the cabin and toward the war-buck.

Joseph took her pack, seemingly deep in thought. "What do they need?" he asked bluntly.

"Need?" she asked, confused by his abrupt change of subject.

"To ensure this baby's survival. To ensure Juberin's milk is sufficient and that she heals well enough to support another child...if they wish it. What do they need?"

Berel stared into his earnest eyes. "You're serious." Her heart skipped.

"They've suffered too much. If I'd known... What do they need, Berel?"

"Better food for Juberin. Doctors for Berisa— at least for half a year, to be safe. Warm clothing and quilts for the autumn and winter to come."

"They have it."

Her breathing hitched and her heart pounded. "You mean it?"

"Will you help me pick the things out later today?"

"Yes." Berel hugged him. "Oh, Joseph! Thank you."

"You know other families in need," he stated, wrapping his arms around her. "Despite my uncle's reforms, there are soldiers who need the basic necessities for their families like Tralean and Juberin do."

"I do." She pulled her head back, meeting his eyes.

"Today," he breathed, bringing his mouth down on hers.

Berel met him passionately, needing his comfort after nearly losing yet another babe from this family. Were it not for Joseph's healing touch, she had no doubt they'd be mourning another dead child...and, perhaps, Juberin as well.

Joseph eased back, nipping at her lips. "I want you," he whispered, his breath heating her lips.

She nodded, mentally calculating how long it would take them to reach the palace and his rooms.

"Let me show you something."

"Yes."

* * * *

Joseph kissed the back of Berel's neck, his fingers straying to the moisture at the apex of her thighs. She squirmed against him, riding his fingertips and teasing his rigid length with each movement.

He pulled the buttons on her trouskit open, reveling in her rising scent. Berel gasped as he slid his hand over her woman's curls, his fingers seeking out her core. Noric's rolling pace created marvelous friction of his fingers within her. It would be so easy to send her over, but he held back, wanting her to want him as desperately as he wanted her.

Berel tangled her fingers in his hair, turning her face up to his and guiding his mouth down. There was nothing gentle about their kiss. It was unleashed, unrestrained, all-consuming. Joseph's cock burned and throbbed for her.

Noric came to a halt, indicating that they'd reached the meadow he sought. Berel drew her leg over Noric's neck, turning sideways across Joseph's lap. She repeated the motion so that she faced him on the buck's back.

Joseph groaned, as she pulled at his trousers, opening the buttons and wrapping her fingers around him. He dragged off his tunic, dropping it to the lush vegetation beneath them.

He slid off Noric's back, drawing Berel with him. Joseph set her on her feet, peeling off her tunic and tossing it away without noting where it landed. Berel smiled at that, pushing her trouskit off and kicking it away. She reached for his trousers, but Joseph held her hands away.

"What is it?" she asked.

"Give this Trial a chance," he requested. "Don't make me struggle to touch you anymore."

She made as if to speak then paused, seemingly uncertain for some reason.

"Would it be so horrible?" he asked. "Would learning you carried my child be—"

"No. It wouldn't." Berel pressed her lips to his chest. "I agree."

"You'll share my bed?" He gathered her to his body. "You won't fight me?"

"Yes. I— No. I won't fight the Trial."

"I'll hold you to that," he warned. Joseph glanced at the hilltop, noting that time was short. There were only a few moments left until sunrise. There was no better way to seal her agreement than with a show of the gods' might.

* * * *

Berel gasped as Joseph swept her to the soft mat of grass, pushing his trousers down his thighs. She hooked her legs over his hips, encouraging a fierce mating.

As if reading her thoughts again, Joseph shook his head. He laced his fingers through hers, easing inside her body. Berel cried out, her entire body trembling in need. Joseph ground his teeth, determination burning in his beautiful eyes. He pulled back, leaving her body entirely, holding her hands down when Berel made to grasp at him.

"Joseph," she begged.

His cock slid inside her, stretching her sheath to accommodate him, band by band. He withdrew again.

"I need you. Please, Joseph."

"You need me?"

She nodded, arching up as he entered her. He captured her mouth as he settled deep inside. Joseph retreated. Berel dragged her mouth from his, a sob escaping her lips.

He didn't give her a chance to beg for his return. She groaned at the feeling of him filling her. Then he was gone again.

"No," she whispered, struggling against his hold, trying to pull him to her with her legs.

"No?" he teased.

"Don't stop. I need you."

His cock lodged deep, stealing her breath. "You need me?" She was abruptly empty, then full again. "Or you need this?"

Berel gasped in understanding.

Joseph left her body. "Say it," he requested. "Which is it that you want?"

She hesitated, unwilling to lie to him, even when her mind argued that it was the prudent course.

The rigid length teased between her labia. "Which? Is this what you want?"

Berel shook her head. "You. I want you."

Joseph filled her, closing his eyes, panting and groaning softly. His cock pulsed inside her. "Then don't push me away again."

His body slid back and forth, driving her to release as the sun topped the hillside. His body stilled, a strangled cry issuing forth from his lips as he erupted inside her.

And then it happened. His cock bit into her

stim band, drowning her body in sensation. The heat and shocks were punctuated by the unmistakable feeling of the gates to her womb opening wide.

The world exploded in color. For an instant, Berel felt certain it was an illusion of some sort, but her mind numbly processed that it was the morning sun on the many flowers around them. Blue burgel, pale gold iri, new pink lizor, orange hurabek, green grasses and tan vines all glowed around her. It was the miracle of birth. The spectacle humbled her.

Joseph's mouth mated with hers, slow and sweet. She let the sensation sweep her away much as the light had swept over the meadow, her mind full of plans. Her research had been fruitful. Now, there was nothing to fear. She could have everything she wanted.

* * * *

"It's too much," Berel argued, half-laughing at his excitement. Given the chance, Joseph would have everything in the store delivered to Juberin...most likely everything in every store they intended to visit. "Juberin couldn't fit this much in her home."

"Perhaps I should arrange for a new home then," he teased.

"You wouldn't dare."

Joseph pressed his body to hers, trapping the Fion blue quilt between them. "Then tell me who else needs these things. I will have them sent somewhere." His voice lowered, sending curls of arousal through her. "Or should I have them sent to the palace?"

Her face heated at the reminder that they might need such a quilt for the presentation of Joseph's heir. "Renia," she forced out. "Luvin...and Zinia will give birth soon."

"Good. I will summon a clerk. You can give the instructions for delivery."

Berel nodded, his proximity scattering her senses. Joseph brushed a kiss over her lips, then strode away. She smiled at his retreating back, running a hand over the quilt.

Her gaze strayed to the many wonderful nursery items. Without a conscious plan, Berel started walking the circumference of the display round. Her fingertips traced the mark of Fion on a cradle, and she stopped to admire the workman's skill. Yes, if she had a child...

Berel sighed and moved on, trying not to dwell on her hopes and dreams. What if she didn't conceive? She glanced to Joseph nervously. If she didn't conceive, he wasn't bound to contract. She could demand him and bind him that way, but if he didn't want her—

He waited for me! He planned to make me his, however he had to. Of course, he wants me.

She pushed away the argument, smiling at a beautiful tapestry, running her hand over the matching quilt. Berel hugged the presentation quilt to her chest, visualizing the nursery she'd build for their child.

"I thought you knew better than this."

Berel startled at the unpleasant voice, turning

to Corin Laes, though she would like to ignore her. One did not ignore a noblewoman.

Corin's face was hard in fury. "You want to destroy him," she accused. "The nobles will not support this. A Keen King has never—"

"You're wrong," Berel answered calmly, turning her attention back to the quilt she liked so much. Yes, if they had a child, this quilt would cover him at night. "In Ti 1-162, Gor Ti contracted with the milk nurse for his daughter and made her queen. She gave him three heirs to the throne. In Ri 2-159, Der Ri contracted—"

"It doesn't matter," Corin snapped. "That is ancient history. What Prince Joseph has to contend with are the nobles of today, not those of millennia ago. Whether or not there is precedent, the nobles will not support a lowborn queen. Of course..." She chuckled, a dangerous sound. "If Joseph wants a romp, an heir from a lowborn mistress, no one would begrudge him a bit of youthful exuberance before he accepts his duty."

Corin ran her gilded nails over the tapestry Berel favored. "Quaint," she commented coolly. "It has its place." She strode away, her head high.

Berel took a calming breath, unfisting her hands and smoothing the wrinkles she'd left in the quilt.

"Your choices, mi'lady?" the clerk asked brightly.

What choice? Berel thought bitterly.

"Of course," she managed in an unwavering voice. "Juberin and Tralean in barracks block number six—"

* * * *

Joseph ran his hands up Berel's silin-covered back, watching her in the mirror. She met his reflected eyes too briefly, smoothing the brush through long, dark tresses that had long before been tamed. He burrowed his hands beneath the thick waves, letting them slide through his fingers, the lightly-scented fall taunting him with the memory of other beckoning places in her body.

"Come to bed." His voice was gruff in need, in the hunger for her that had plagued him for the better part of a decade.

Berel nodded, turning from the mirror, her eyes not quite meeting his. He bit back a sigh of frustration at that, following her to the edge of the bed. She'd been distant since he'd left her in the nursery shop that morning, and he had no idea why.

He'd been gone less than a quarter of an hour, giving the clerk his instructions and collecting a tray of food and drinks from the inn two doors down for them to allow her time to do what he'd asked. The clerk's smile and nod at his return had let Joseph know that she'd done her work well, spying on Berel from afar in his absence and noting the things Berel favored for her own. For a moment, he'd known nothing but satisfaction for an accomplishment that held meaning for him...for them as a couple.

Then he'd handed Berel a lizor freeze, and confusion had set in. Berel hadn't met his eyes fully from that moment until this. She'd tried to feign distraction with the tasks of the day, but Berel had never been a competent liar. She hadn't shied from his touch, but her smiles were strained and her manner distant, as if her heart were closed off to him again.

Joseph turned her to him, raising her chin to draw Berel's eyes to his. He expected fear—perhaps guilt or nervousness or confusion. The longing in her eyes stole his breath. He cupped both hands behind her head, closing his eyes to the feeling of her mouth opening to his. Her hands traced the line of curls down his chest to the tie of his lounging pants. Joseph groaned as the silin slid over his hips to pool at his feet.

He kissed her chin, lifting it further to seek out the well of musk at her throat. "Anything," he offered. "Tell me what you want, Berel."

Her hand brushed over the sensitive tip of his cock. "I want to taste you."

He shivered in delight at that. How many nights had he dreamed of Berel's mouth as schente drank him down? *Too many.* "Yes," he whispered. "Taste me."

Berel looked at the bed, uncertain. Joseph smiled at her inexperience. He settled in the center of the bed, stacking pillows behind his back for comfort, his legs parted in invitation.

She knelt between his knees, her eyes locked on his rigid length. Joseph forced his eyes open, as she played her fingers over the nerve bundle just below the head, finding the erogenous zone effortlessly.

He could almost hear her reciting the lessons she and her mother had given his sisters, starting

173

at age fourteen: the ways to pleasure a man, the ways he would pleasure her, and the traditions and laws dealing with mating and contracts. His own lessons had not been entirely different, though his duties to his chosen partners had been stressed...and very little of his instruction had come from a woman healer, while most of Jenneane's had.

She lowered her head, running her nose through the curls that surrounded his cock, her lips brushing softly over his length. Joseph groaned, fisting his hands in restraint when he wanted to pull her down onto him, bury himself in her heat.

"Am I—" she began.

"More," he breathed, tangling his hands in her hair.

Berel's tongue caressed the head, stealing a bit of his essence. Her eyes closed in pleasure. She took the head into the heat of her mouth.

"Merciful Fion." Joseph's voice rasped from a mouth gone abruptly dry. "Mag alive."

Encouraged by his outburst, Berel took more of him in. He guided her, watching his length disappearing into Berel's willing body as if hypnotized by the sight. Joseph had never watched a woman fellate him before. With his schente, he'd always closed his eyes and imagined Berel. His imagination was a pale dream in comparison to the truth of having her.

She became bold, taking more of him—faster, deeper, her movements fevered, groaning around him at the first spurt of his early fluids.

"Soon, Berel," he gasped. "Your taste is—"

As if the thought excited her, she took him deep into her mouth and stilled. Joseph's hands tightened in her hair, and he cried out harshly, his seed coursing into her.

Berel made an inarticulate sound, her eyes closing in a look of rapture as she swallowed his release. Joseph thickened, muttering entreaties to Berel and Fion both as he filled her mouth with his increased girth. It was a long few moments of tension before he lessened. He sighed, then chuckled in relief.

Joseph smiled as Berel pressed her lips to his stomach...then to his chest, rising up before him on her knees. He dipped his fingers between her folds, evaluating her heavy-lidded eyes and swollen, drenched core. She gasped, lowering herself over them.

"Ten times more powerful when taken internally," he reminded her.

She rocked her hips against his hand, her breathing ragged. He guided his fingers out of her, and she shook her head, biting her lip as she watched him raise them to sample her musk.

"Ten times..." he breathed, his erection renewing that simply.

Berel leaned forward and pushed up on her knees, pressing her lips to his, trembling against his body. She pulled her knees out and forward, one at a time, straddling his hips, riding the ridge of his cock.

Joseph prepared himself to forego more if she were uncertain about completion. "Are you sure—"

She sealed her mouth to his, guiding her sheath around him. Berel met his thrusts, grinding hard against him, her kiss verging on desperation.

It ended all too quickly. Joseph cradled Berel to his chest, noting her silence in rising unease.

"What is it?" he asked. "What is wrong?"

"Just hold me," she requested. "Just for tonight."

"Forever," he vowed. "For as long as you'll have me."

Berel didn't answer him, leaving Joseph to wonder yet again what had gone wrong.

CHAPTER SIXTEEN

Endl 23ʳᵈ, Ri 25-3010

"So, why are you really here?" Jenneane asked.

Berel stiffened, weighing her friendship with Neane against the princess's dedication to her twin. "No reason," she lied.

"How long have we known each other, Berel?"

"My mother tells a story of you and Joseph stealing me from my cradle to play with Eve. You— I suppose you've always been there."

"And you think you can lie to me? You've never been able to lie." Jenneane ran a hand over her growing womb, looking content.

Berel wished she felt half as settled. "As if you are a master deceiver," she countered.

"No changing the subject."

"I..." Berel rubbed her temple, searching for a way to explain it. "I can't lie to you. Can I?"

"No, and I can't understand why you would hesitate to tell me the truth. Have I ever told your secrets?"

"I don't recall *having* any secrets."

"What about the time you, Rebecca, and Rolin overturned the supply transport full of baking supplies?"

Berel winced. "All right. I can trust you." *I hope.*

Jenneane didn't give her a chance to consider how to approach the subject. "Why are you pushing Joseph away? You've wanted him forever."

"Am I that translucent?"

"Like a clear, blue sky. Not even a cloud. Not even—"

Berel groaned at that.

"Be reasonable, Berel. Anyone with eyes has known how you two have felt about each other for years. It's been nearly killing Joseph to know it and not be able to do anything about it."

"You knew he intended this and didn't warn me?"

"Well, not the specifics. No. I thought he'd just ask you and be done with it. Of course, I thought you'd just agree and be done with it. But...yes, I knew he intended to convince you to a contract when you were an adult."

"Why didn't I ever see this?"

"Didn't you?"

Berel considered that. Had she ever really believed it, or had it always been an unobtainable fantasy?

"Why did you start pushing him away? I can mark the day, Berel. Just tell me why."

"I can't do this to him, Jenneane," she managed miserably.

"This? What exactly is *this*?"

"Joseph has trained all his life to be king. He loves his diplomatic work. I can't take that away from him."

"Why would you ask him to give it up?" she asked in confusion.

"I wouldn't! I can't. I can't contract with him. Don't you see?" Berel shook her head, at a loss to outline such a complex problem in few enough words to satisfy the princess who never sat still for a moment.

Jenneane's eyes narrowed. "I don't think I understand. What does contracting with you have to do with Joseph's future as king?"

"The nobles want one of their daughters as queen." Berel watched Jenneane's shifting emotions, hardly breathing, her hands clasped in her lap.

"Someone told you this?" Jenneane asked carefully.

"More than one," she admitted. "Apparently, I am easier to read than I care to consider."

Jenneane darkened. "How dare they," she exploded.

Berel grimaced. "Please, calm down. This isn't—"

"Good for me or my babe. I know. Tirin is fond of pointing that out to me."

"You do this often?"

"Don't change the subject."

"As your woman healer—"

"You're not my woman healer today."

"I'm always—"

"Berel! You are losing the man you love for this petty *bullshit*. Forget about my temper for a moment."

She nodded, her stomach rolling at the truth of the matter.

"Tell me who said it."

"Why? So they can die a ritual death? Would you kill every noble, just so Joseph and I can contract?"

"Don't tempt me," she muttered.

Berel cracked a smile at that. If they got Eve in on this discussion, the nobles wouldn't stand a chance. "I thought Tirin had leashed your temper."

Jenneane laughed. "Only between ourselves. Oh, you did it again. You need to tell Joseph about this."

Berel's head spun at Jenneane's jumps from topic to topic. "I can't. You know Joseph. You know what he'll do." *Actually, I don't know what he'll do, but he won't be easy to deal with.*

She nodded. "You really think the nobles would carry it that far?"

"I know they would."

Jenneane sipped at an implin freeze, seemingly deep in thought. "I still think you should tell Joseph...but you won't do that. If you want my opinion, and I assume you do, because you're here."

"You make me dizzy," Berel complained.

"I just give you a lot to think about."

"What is your opinion?" she asked weakly.

"Take the contract."

"But, the nobles will—"

"Will find a united front in the royal family. A king may need the support of the nobles to rule, but how can the nobles fight us all? Take the contract, give Joseph an heir, and they won't have any grounds to contest it."

Berel considered that. She rose, ambling to the door with a vague note of thanks.

"Think about it," Jenneane called after her.

"I will."

Berel wandered out to the closest balcony,

staring past the medicinal plants. What would it take to defeat the nobles? If she contracted with Joseph, would they dare challenge him?

An image of Corin flashed into her mind. Corin would challenge the marriage out of pure spite. What would it take to make them retreat?

Give Joseph an heir.

"A child," she whispered. Even the king couldn't use non-allowance if they'd produced a child. The Breeding Office and the Church Council would back the royal family. And, as Jenneane had noted, the royal family would stand together. The nobles wouldn't dare challenge Joseph then.

Berel strode to Joseph's office, her mind spinning with plans. She had fifteen days left to conceive. If she carried a child before the end of the Trial Moon, she'd contract with Joseph and trust that the combined pressure would be enough to keep the nobles leashed.

If she didn't conceive... She swallowed hard at that, blinking back tears. If she didn't conceive, it would be the royal family alone against the nobles. Berel couldn't think about that. She refused to consider what she'd do.

She pushed open the door to Joseph's office, stepped inside, and closed it behind her, snapping the lock shut. His head came up. Joseph looked to the door in confusion, setting his pen down and meeting her eyes.

"Berel? Is something wrong?"

She shook her head, peeling off the silin day dress and dropping it to the floor.

Joseph didn't question that. He rose from behind his desk, shedding his uniform jacket onto his chair and dragging his tunic off before he reached her.

Berel laid a hand on his bare chest, feeling his heart pounding behind his ribs. She pressed her body to his, laying teasing kisses over his jaw and throat, gasping in delight as he pulled his trousers open. Joseph lifted her slightly, pressed her to the wall, and pierced her body in one savage thrust.

CHAPTER SEVENTEEN

Endl 36th, Ri 25-3010

Joseph pulled Berel into his arms, uneasy though he couldn't say why. He tried reasoning that the approaching end of Trial unnerved him, but it wasn't that simple.

From the day Berel had come to his office, she had been a passionate lover, never shying from Joseph's touch, seeking him out for stolen moments so often that his father sent him knowing glances at almost every private meeting. In light of that, his unease made little sense. Logically, he should be anticipating the end of Trial for her automatic agreement to be his bride.

Was it that she hadn't asked to contract? She didn't have to wait for the end of Trial. If she intended to stay, why hadn't she asked to sign it already? Was the fact that she hadn't done so a sign that she still intended to leave him?

Was it that they never discussed their future together? That Berel never met his eyes, when he strayed onto the subject?

She stroked a hand up his inner thigh, massaging the nerve bundle behind his sac with a sly smile.

Joseph groaned. "You will pay for that," he warned her.

"Will I?" Her other hand stimulated the cluster below the head, forcing the release of a few drops of his fluids.

He fought the urge to spend in her hand. Joseph started tracing the bel tro, smiling at her shiver of acceptance. "You will."

The next few minutes were an unhurried battle, each of them playing on the arousal of the other. Joseph employed every scrap of self-control he possessed, determined to outlast her.

Berel straightened her legs, tipping her hips in an unconscious attempt to urge his fingers into her. Her moans mixed with his, and she fisted one hand in his hair as Joseph suckled at her breast. She gasped his name, pleading for him.

"Yes, my love?" he replied innocently.

"Don't tease me." She moved her hands to his shoulders, guiding him toward her.

He held back. "Promise me anything," he bargained.

She met his gaze, abruptly wary, her arousal lessening before his eyes. "I—I can't."

"You don't trust me?"

Berel darkened. "Of course, I do."

"Then promise me anything." How often had he promised her as much? Why couldn't she return the favor?

"I...can't." Again, she wouldn't meet his eyes.

Joseph bit back a curse at that. Every time he thought he was making progress, every time he thought he'd won Berel as his own, his hopes were crushed.

He pushed from the bed, his need to distance himself overpowering. Wanting her, giving Berel all he could with no discernable return, was likely to drive him insane. He pulled on a pair of lounging pants, tying them in clipped motions of his hands.

"Joseph?" She barely whispered his name, her voice choked.

He didn't answer. Joseph wasn't certain his voice would issue forth if he tried.

"Where are you going?"

"I don't know." He strode to the door and out into the corridor.

He didn't know where he was going. Joseph wasn't entirely certain that he cared. For all it mattered, he could walk to the stables, unclothed as he was, and the stares of others wouldn't make a difference to him. What did it matter where he went if he wasn't with Berel?

He found himself at the door to Jenneane's rooms. Of course, he came here. If anyone could help him see clearly, it was his twin. She probably understood his upset better than he did. Joseph hesitated for a moment then knocked lightly, praying that Neane was taking the late morning rest Syl had ordered while she carried.

Neane opened the door. She met his eyes, and her welcoming smile disappeared. "Joseph?"

"I need to talk to you." They'd never made a habit of walking on eggshells around each other, as their mother would say; this was no exception to that rule.

She nodded and waved him in, placing a hand over her growing child. Joseph sighed at that. He'd dreamed of Berel carrying his child. At this rate, she'd walk away from the contract...and him before he had a chance to see it.

Neane settled on the edge of her bed. "What is it, Joseph?"

"I'm losing her," he admitted bluntly.

"Berel?" Her eyes widened in surprise.

Joseph nodded, sinking into a chair and planting his forehead in his hands.

"I thought things were going well," she noted in confusion.

"Sexually, they are. Actually...most of it is going well." Why was this so hard to explain?

"Then I don't understand the problem."

Joseph stared at her, at a loss to put his unease into words. "Berel..." He grumbled a curse. "She never discusses the future, Neane. I feel..." He motioned his hand uncertainly.

"You don't think she sees a future with you." She didn't ask it.

He gaped at her, trying to unravel her strange insight into his life. "Yes. No. I don't know what she thinks. She—"

"Do you really think she'd refuse you?"

"I don't know, and the uncertainty is driving me out of my mind."

"Where is Berel?"

He shook his head. Who knew where she was by now? Chances were she'd dressed as quickly as she could after he left and retreated to her storeroom or the barracks...anywhere he wasn't.

"Joseph?" Her voice was sharp and insistent.

"I don't know, Neane. I don't know where she is."

"You walked away from her. Didn't you?"

He nodded miserably.

"*Idiot male fuck,*" she cursed fluently in English.

Joseph winced. Neane had only used that particular term on one other male that he knew of.

If she used it now, it was a safe bet that he'd screwed up royally. He winced again at the unintended pun.

"How could you," she shouted.

"Being upset—"

"If you *dare* tell me it's not good for my babe, I vow I will take my dagger to you."

"My mistake was that big?" he asked sheepishly. Joseph knew it was. He shouldn't have left her that way.

Neane crossed her arms over her chest, glaring at him.

"What can I do, Jenneane?" he pleaded. "I am doing everything I can. What am I missing? What more can I do?"

She seemed torn. "Talk to her."

"What?" Hadn't he been trying to talk to her? That was the problem, after all. She wouldn't talk to him about their future.

"Something is— Berel has to have a reason, Joseph. Find out what it is. If you want her to contract with you—"

"You know I do."

"Then talk to her."

Joseph nodded, standing with a sigh. "Thanks, Neane."

"Don't thank me. Go talk to your bride."

He smiled weakly. If only he could trust that Berel would be his bride in the end, he might not be half-mad now.

Joseph headed back to his rooms, planning his search pattern. No matter what, he would have to dress before he started out. Walking around the private areas of the palace at this time of day in his sleeping clothes was shocking enough. Despite his upset, he couldn't do more than that. He opened the door, then stilled inside, staring in disbelief.

He'd thought she would run from him at her first opportunity. She hadn't. Berel was dressed but seated on the bed, her hands clasped in her lap. She didn't look at him or offer any comment. For a long moment, Joseph wasn't sure she knew he was there.

He didn't approach her. If he did that, he might forget that they had to talk. "I'm sorry," he offered.

She squeezed her eyes shut. "I can't, Joseph. I wish I could, but—"

"Don't. I shouldn't have demanded anything. The Trial Moon isn't about force. I know that."

Berel peeked up at him, seemingly tortured by something he couldn't name but wished he could.

Joseph went to her, settling onto the bed next to her, touching her cheek. "I shouldn't have walked away from you. I wasn't thinking."

She leaned toward him, pressing her lips to his cheek. "Please, don't," she whispered.

"Berel, why did—"

Her lips met his, trembling lightly. "Joseph," she pleaded.

Talk to her. I should talk to her.

Berel turned toward him fully, pressing her hands to his chest, finding the well of musk above his nipple and massaging it. Her mouth was urgent against his, and her hands worked at the tie to his lounging pants. He groaned as she tasted the well of his musk, fueling his arousal and her own with it. His resolve shattered, he pulled up at her dress.

Talking could wait. Joseph lost himself in a frenzy of touching and tasting. Clothing was tossed aside. Mouths meshed, then explored, returning to kiss again. Hands kneaded and stroked. Voices rose and fell in a chorus of sighs and moans, pleas and assurances.

They cried out together as Joseph filled her. Her body was hot and tight, her muscles spasming around his length. Berel wrapped her legs around him, meeting Joseph on each thrust.

She came quickly, and Joseph followed. He muttered a prayer to Fion, begging the blessing of a child from this union. Gods help him, it might be the only way to hold her if he didn't get to the bottom of whatever reservations she had.

Joseph laid his cheek to Berel's, stroking his lips up to hers. He felt at home, buried within her as he'd always known he should be.

"Berel, we need—"

She shook her head. "As much as I can," she whispered. "You have my vow on that."

His heart ached at the hesitancy in her voice. "I won't ask for promises," he assured her. "Not today." Joseph pushed away the thought that Berel would have to make a decision for or against him in two more days. Surely, two days was enough time to find out what troubled her.

CHAPTER EIGHTEEN

Wos 1ˢᵗ, Ri 25-3010

Joseph held his breath as Syl led Berel into his father's office. Berel didn't look his direction. He bit back a groan of agony at that. Either she was carrying and unhappy about contracting with him, or she had made a decision that she wasn't happy about. Nothing was certain.

Unless she carried. Joseph begged Fion again for that favor. It seemed he'd been begging her for it for the last week of his life. All he needed was the time the Trial Moon contract would win him to convince her properly, perhaps to convince her to tell him what she kept hidden away from him so carefully.

"Your determination?" his father asked Syl.

She flicked an apologetic look at Joseph. "There is no cap."

"Stay," Joseph asked, not quite pleading with Berel. If there was no cap, she had chosen to leave him. He didn't question it.

"Joseph," his father warned. He turned to Berel. "You can still ask for the contract. If you refuse, you must present yourself to Syl in one week's time to—to prove you don't carry."

She nodded, swallowing what looked to be a knot of tears. Berel looked around at his assembled family, the same ones that were present at the start of this. Neane was the only person whose eyes she met for longer than a moment, and even then, she looked away. She stared at the floor before her boots, seemingly fighting for speech.

"Berel?" Jole prodded her. "What is your decision?"

"I can't," she whispered. "I—I'm sorry." Berel bolted for the door.

Joseph surged after her, calling for her to stop, desperate for a chance to convince her to change her mind before it was too late to undo what she'd just done.

"Joseph," his father barked.

Tirin stepped between Joseph and the doorway, shaking his head as a sign that he wouldn't let him pursue Berel further.

"By the law of—" Jole began in a gruff voice.

"*Fuck the law*," Joseph exploded in English. He sank to the floor with his back to the shelves full of tomes of history and law—useless texts that hadn't worked as he'd needed them to. Joseph buried his face in his hands.

His father's hand closed on his shoulder. "You have to let her go, Joseph."

Joseph shook him off and pushed to his feet, shouldering past Tirin and heading for the main stairs.

"Joseph!"

"Don't worry. I won't disgrace you, Father," he growled.

Joseph didn't wait for an answer to that. He went to his rooms, staring at the bed miserably. Finally, he took a spare quilt from the cabinet and curled onto the lounging couch. The faint smell of Berel permeated the entire room, taunting him, a reminder of his greatest failure...the only failure that really counted.

"I vowed never to fail you," he whispered. "How did I fail you?"

* * * *

Joseph groaned at the sound of a knock at his door. "Go away," he grumbled.

"Joseph," Neane called. "May I enter?"

He considered sending her away, but a need to see her stilled his tongue. "Come in, Neane."

She let herself in and met his eyes, seemingly pained by the sight of him. "Oh, Joseph," she exclaimed, closing the door and coming to his side.

Joseph wanted to assure her that he'd be fine, but the lie stuck in his throat. He shook his head, trusting that his twin would understand as she always had before.

She shifted nervously. "It's not you she's running from," she confided.

"You knew she'd leave me?" he asked, his voice as hollow as his heart.

"Mag's Honor, no," she gasped. "I thought..." Jenneane started twisting the curl above her ear, casting a pained look at him.

Joseph scowled. "You thought what?"

"I thought she'd talk to you. I told her to talk to you...and you to talk to her, for Mother's sake. I thought that together—"

"About what?"

Jenneane darkened. "I gave my vow. If I could

have told you, don't you think I would have by now?"

"Jenneane," he warned.

She winced. "I gave my vow."

"How am I supposed to win her back if I don't know what I am fighting?" he demanded.

"You need to talk to Berel. I told you that you needed to talk to her."

"And how am I supposed to do that, Jenneane?"

She sighed. "I don't know," she admitted. "I just know that Berel needs you as much as you need her."

Joseph considered that. Until Berel refused him, he would have sworn that it was true, but she *had* refused him. "How did I fail her?" he grumbled.

"You didn't. I told you—"

"I know. I have to talk to Berel." He sighed.

"No. She's not running from you."

He ground his teeth in frustration at the half-answers he was getting. "And you're not going to tell me what she *is* running from."

"I told you—"

"I know," he snapped. "Damn Mag for this."

"Will you come to dinner?" Jenneane asked. "You've refused to leave your—couch all day."

"I don't think I'm ready to hold a civil conversation with our father yet," he apologized. "And...I'm really not very hungry."

Jenneane's eyes glittered, a sure sign she was up to mischief. A smile pulled up at her lips. "Oh, you needn't face *Daddy*."

Joseph levered himself up to sitting, his

interest piqued. "Has he gone somewhere?" Considering Joseph's volatile state, it hardly seemed like something Jole would do.

"Of course not." She smiled wider.

"Then what—"

"Really, Joseph," she chided him, rolling her green eyes. "Is the dining room the only place you will deign to eat?"

His mind whirled as her plan unfolded for him. He launched off of the lounging couch, laughing, kissing Neane on the cheek with a rushed word of thanks. Joseph went about his toilet as quickly as he could then launched into the now-empty bedroom to dress. Looking passably kept in a soft pair of trousers, tunic, and boots, he practically sprinted to the kitchen.

The cooks scrambled to their feet as he strolled through the door, and Joseph waved them away. He served himself a plate from the stove, ignoring the scandalized expressions on servants' faces as best he could.

Vila, the house head, approached as he took a seat at the long table. "If you wish a tray," she hinted.

"This is perfect," Joseph assured her.

Vila's eyes widened in shock. "If you require anything, Your Highness—"

"I have everything I require," he lied smoothly, offering the gray-haired woman a wink and a smile. "Would you care to join me?"

"Uh...I—I mean, no, Your Highness."

Joseph sampled the portrain stew that was the servants' fare for evening meal. "You should try this, House Head Vila. It is excellent."

The old woman gasped at his familiar form of address. "Are you quite well, Your Highness?"

He stilled with the spoon halfway to his mouth, noting the murmur of voices around him growing louder. Joseph raised his eyes slowly. Berel stood in the doorway, grasping at the frame as if she were faint.

"Quite well, Vila," he whispered, placing the spoon back in the bowl, his hunger overwhelmed by the fluttering in his stomach at the sight of Berel.

The old woman turned to face Berel, then swung to Joseph, her eyes wide and wild.

"Leave me," he ordered in a voice low enough to escape other ears.

She retreated, barely noted by Joseph.

He held Berel's gaze, unwilling to allow her to escape him easily. She edged back as if she would bolt from him again, and he tensed to pursue. Berel planted her feet, seemingly determined to hold her ground against him.

"You should not be here," she managed, her voice strained.

"It is my home as well as yours," he reasoned pleasantly.

"You cannot be here," Berel insisted, on the verge of panic.

"I am, and I am not leaving until we have a discussion. Here, in my office, with Jenneane as witness, if you wish. Mark me, Berel, we will discuss this."

"There is nothing to discuss."

"You said that once before, and you were incorrect then, as well."

"The law says—"

"Have I touched you?" he challenged.

She shook her head.

Joseph forced his voice to gentle. "I'm right here, Berel. You cannot chase me away. You cannot send me away. I'm not leaving."

"Then I am." She turned on her heel and started down the corridor toward her rooms.

He rose from the table, knocking his chair to the floor as he strode to the corridor. Joseph followed her, determined to speak to her, whatever it took. "Why are you running from me?" he pleaded. "What has you so frightened?"

Berel turned to him at the door, tears marring her cheeks, tears he would be sanctioned for soothing away. "You have to stop," she whispered.

"Contract with me. Sign a real contract. Not a Trial Moon. I'm offering it, Berel. I would have offered it at any time. Don't you know that?"

Her face paled, and she shook her head frantically.

"You belong with me. You know—"

"No. I don't. I—I have a place, Joseph."

"A place?" he repeated in disgust. "Have I ever treated you that way?"

"No." She turned and eased through the door to the rooms she shared with her mother.

He braced it open with his hand, unwilling to leave it at that. "You are the most important thing in my life," he informed her. "You are the only important thing to me."

Berel closed her eyes, looking pained. "You were born to a destiny, Joseph. That destiny is not mine. I cannot be your queen."

"Berel—"

"Please, leave me." She pushed at the door.

Joseph moved his hand and allowed her to close and lock it. "I will not be dismissed. I love you, Berel."

She didn't answer him, but neither did he hear the sound of her boots retreating across the stone floors behind the door.

"I do love you," he whispered, knowing she could hear him.

He ambled away, furious with himself. He had no more information now than he'd started with, and talking to Berel wasn't solving that.

"Seven days," he grumbled. If he didn't convince Berel in seven days, she'd be gone from his life forever. But how could he convince her, when the law decreed that he couldn't touch her?

CHAPTER NINETEEN

Wos 2nd, Ri 25-3010

"You cannot spend the rest of the week in this room," Syl commented for the third time in a day.

Berel grumbled a curse, rubbing a shaking hand over her aching skull. "Are you refusing to help me?"

"I didn't raise a coward."

"Fine. I'll get my own food," she replied stubbornly. *And bring it directly back here...as soon as I develop an appetite again.* Just the thought of facing Joseph made her stomach cramp uncomfortably.

Her mother stared at Berel, her arms crossed over her ample chest and her head cocked to one side. "You're determined to push him away?"

Something dark and dangerous rose up in her. "It is my choice, Mother." At least...if she dared choose, she would have the choice of leaving him.

"So it is." Syl seemed to consider that carefully. "Very well. I will bring your meals to you and take on the duties that will be mine when you leave."

Berel closed her eyes, pulling the quilt tighter around her body, exhausted. "Thank you."

"I will bring you a calming tea with your meal. Your upset isn't healthy. You'll get ill."

I'm already getting ill. She nodded weakly. The stress of the week of test was wearing at her, and it would only get worse if she had to face Joseph again.

Syl pushed the hair from Berel's forehead. "Just remember one thing," she cautioned.

"What?" Berel mumbled, sleep calling to her, drowning out the world.

"Mother Fion does not often allow us to run from the gifts she offers. You are but a woman who balks the gods. Never forget that."

Berel nodded, though she couldn't make much sense of that comment.

* * * *

Joseph stared at Syl in frustration, fighting down the urge to flip the tray laden with food she carried. His heart sank. There was no reason for Berel to leave her hiding place if Syl brought her food. There was no way to convince Berel to stay.

Syl offered him a strained smile. "Don't lose hope," she advised him.

"You'll help me?" he asked, his body too stiff in his attempt not to show his nervousness. "You'll stop carrying her food and force Berel to face me?"

Her voice was solemn. "That is something I cannot do."

Joseph bit back pure fury. Everyone seemed determined to help Berel avoid him. His father and Tirin were watching him closely, quoting the damned laws of Trial Moon at every turn. Jenneane still refused to tell him whatever Berel had confided in her. Now Syl was allowing her to hide from him. He'd lost his last possible ally.

"Then there is nothing left to hope for," he growled.

"Joseph—"

"I cannot convince a shadow, Syl," he all but shrieked at her.

"I don't believe you will have to convince her. In time, I think Berel will come to see the futility of running from you."

"Will you at least tell me why?" he pleaded, losing all sense of pride and decorum. "Why is she afraid to contract with me?"

"If I knew why, I'd tell you. You have my word on that."

"Then why are you letting her play this game?" he demanded.

Syl managed a more natural smile that time. "Some lessons should be painful."

"And what lesson am I supposed to learn?" Surely, he'd felt enough pain by now to satisfy her.

"Did I imply the lesson was yours to learn?" she countered smoothly. Syl raised an eyebrow in what Joseph was sure was supreme amusement. "My apologies, Joseph. That was not my intent."

"Is it a lesson Berel has to learn?" he asked bluntly, weary of games.

"Most assuredly." Her tone was one of commiseration, fellowship, perhaps even conspiracy.

Joseph started to smile. It faded with the realization that Syl said it would be a painful lesson. His anger and frustration aside, he didn't want Berel hurt. "How painful a lesson will it be?" he asked, hoping she'd read the warning in his voice.

"I'll make sure it's not too painful for her. You have my solemn vow of that, but ultimately, Berel will decide when she's had enough. It is her choice to end her pain."

"Then she can still leave me," he grumbled. "Pain can be conquered."

Syl chuckled. "Do you pray to Fion, Joseph?"

He darkened, nodding in response.

"Remember who Berel serves."

The woman healers had always been called the servants of Fion. The early Ri histories indicated that their knowledge was imparted by the Goddess herself, though historians claimed the information was more of a parable than fact. "What has that—"

"Appease the Mistress of the house," she whispered. Syl looked toward the far corridor meaningfully. "I will send you something soothing this afternoon."

Joseph stared the way she'd motioned, mentally calculating her intent. The sanctum was the opposite direction. Syl wasn't suggesting he simply pray. That corridor held the great lounge and the library.

"A book," he guessed. Joseph snapped his head around to ask Syl which book he sought, but she had already departed with the tray for Berel.

He made his way to the library, considering the improbability of finding a single volume amidst the thousands in the room. "If it takes all week," he vowed. But what was he looking for?

Appease the Mistress of the house. Typically, Joseph would interpret the Mistress of the house to mean his mother, but when discussing Berel's service, he decided Fion was the Mistress Syl meant. But which book? The gods were integral to most aspects of Keen life.

Joseph scanned his eyes over the rows of books with a swirl of apprehension in his gut. *Be logical,* he calmed himself.

Laws were unlikely. Joseph knew the laws. There was nothing in there about appeasing gods. Religious texts full of ancient stories were no better, nor were histories. He knew them all. As heir apparent, Joseph had intensive training in many areas of study.

And it all failed me.

He pushed away that bitter thought and moved on. Religious discussion books were a possibility, especially those that dealt with Fion's Priestesses. Philosophy was likely useless.

He almost passed by the books on trades, but a flash of color caught his eye. Joseph walked toward the length of Fion blue cloth draped over the spine of a book, breathless in anticipation. Had Syl marked the volume for him?

Joseph pushed the silin aside, biting back a laugh of relief. It was a book on the ancient traditions of woman healers. He took the book from the shelf and hurried toward his rooms, hoping it held something to aid him in his quest for Berel.

"Joseph."

He came to a halt, his smile disappearing. Joseph had avoided any conversation of length with his father since Berel had refused the contract. He tucked the book under his arm, hiding the spine.

"Yes, Father?" he asked calmly.

"You're not haunting corridors again, are you?" Jole didn't have to state the rest, the reminder that Joseph wasn't permitted to chase after Berel, the penalties in store if he did.

"Just doing some reading," he replied in half-truth, his manner brusque.

"I know you wanted—"

"What I wanted is immaterial," he snapped. *What I want is all that matters.*

Jole sighed. "Losing a mate is never easy."

Joseph laughed harshly. "As if you'd know. Uncle Michael abducting your bride is hardly comparable to the one I chose leaving me for her own reasons."

"I am trying to offer my support," Jole grumbled.

"You're offering your sympathy. That is something I do not want. I prefer to work this out on my own."

"As you wish. If you want to discuss it—"

"I won't." *Not with you. As maddening as it is, Neane and Syl are much more helpful—perhaps because I know they are on my side.*

Jole nodded and turned away.

Joseph took a calming breath and continued on to his rooms. He shut the door behind him, then opened the book to the page the silin marked. He read the chapter header three times, his smile spreading in understanding.

Syl was much more his ally in gaining Berel than she'd pretended to be. If this information was any indication of her willingness to help him, Berel would soon be near mad for him.

He sobered. Berel was a woman healer too. Would she recognize the deception and put a stop to it? Would she turn him over to his father for punishment? Would she walk away from him in her fury?

Does it matter? This is your only chance to win her back.

Joseph sighed. Of course, it didn't matter that it carried a risk. The risk of losing her was the worst thing that could happen, and it would happen if he did nothing.

He scanned the first few pages, chuckling. There were so many useful ideas, it was hard to choose which to try first. Perhaps he should have a special tray made up for Berel's evening meal.

No. That would be moving too fast. A flower was best. He'd start with an early iri blossom for Berel's tray—a blossom with a special gift for her.

Four hours later, Joseph met Syl in the corridor. He placed the bloom in its vase on the tray of food with a slight bow of his head.

Syl raised an eyebrow at the move. "Chapter three?" she asked patiently.

Joseph bit back a smile. "Oh, yes."

"Excellent choice." She left without a backward glance.

He returned to his rooms, humming an Earth tune that Berel loved, the one they'd danced to all those years ago.

Joseph settled on the couch and flipped open the book, planning for the days to come. "Chapter three," he laughed. "Aphrodisiacs For Drawing Your True Mate To You." True, it was written for drawing a man to a woman, but changing from one gender to the other was easily accomplished.

CHAPTER TWENTY

Wos 6th, Ri 25-3010

"Len be damned," Berel cursed. "It isn't fair. It simply isn't fair."

She needed to eat; if she didn't, her pregnancy signs would worsen, but everything around her put her in mind of Joseph. Even now, she imagined his musk.

Her schen was maddening, and knowing Joseph slept two floors above her made it all the worse. It would be so easy to climb the stairs and slip between his silin sheets to find his hard—

Berel shook away that thought. How could Fion punish her this way? Was it too much to ask that she have a cap at the end of the Trial? It would have been a simple thing to turn to Joseph then.

Now... Berel sighed, pressing a hand to her womb. Joseph hadn't pursued her past that single encounter in the kitchen.

Maybe Jole warned him away, she consoled herself. Just because he didn't pursue her didn't mean he didn't want to.

No. Joseph had never been one to follow orders blindly. If he truly wanted her, he would have found a way to see her again...to press his case.

She pulled a quilt around her shoulders, chilled by more than her pregnancy signs. What if Joseph no longer wanted her? What if his absence meant that he'd moved on and chosen a woman the nobles would approve of?

He is bound, that damned rational part of her mind argued. *By the laws of Trial Moon, he must contract, because you carry his child. Until the week of test is over, he cannot legally petition another woman to a contract.*

Berel shook her head miserably. Did she really want to win him that way?

No. Not that way.

She had to find out if Joseph wanted her without bringing his duty into it. *How will I do that? And, what will I do, if he doesn't want me?*

"I will not contract with a man who doesn't want me," she vowed.

Neither would she accept payment for producing Joseph's heir. Berel groaned. Again, how could she avoid it? By the laws of Trial Moon, Joseph would present her with a stipend when one of them dissolved the contract—less if she dissolved it, but still more than she wanted for giving him a child.

Giving him a child... Berel felt her stomach lurch at that. If either of them dissolved the contract, she had no rights to the babe. She pressed her hands to her womb, her breathing harsh at the thought. "No." Her voice was strangled. She couldn't lose her child.

The child was never truly yours, her mind taunted her. Berel stifled a sob into her hand at that. If Joseph refused her, she'd lose more than her heart in the bargain. "Damn the Trial Moon." She reminded herself to keep her voice low, so her mother wouldn't overhear her.

Her mind raced ahead, coloring a bleak future. If Joseph dissolved the contract, she would have nothing. Not him, not the babe—only the money for her trouble that she didn't want.

Berel forced her heart to calm, offering assurances based on what she knew of Joseph.

Had he ever hurt anyone in spite?

No, but he would in vengeance. When Lord Byen attacked Jenneane, Joseph would have called him to a ritual death if Jole hadn't done so. Berel had heard him say as much in those long days between the attack and when Jole made his decision.

Would he revenge himself for her refusal, taking their child?

Logically. Think logically.

Would Joseph take their child, knowing it would hurt her?

The Trial Moon had been designed to capture Berel as his mate, but what if Joseph no longer wanted a life with her? Not wanting Berel didn't mean he wouldn't want his son...or his re-bred daughter.

Joseph would have to lay claim to his heir. The nobles would demand it. The Church Council and Breeding Office would likely demand it. His father would certainly order it. By the laws of Trial Moon, she couldn't stop that. Even if she ran, there was Human Rejection Syndrome to consider. Hugam was essential to her life and their child's.

Not that she could realistically hide from him. With the heir to the Keen throne at stake, there was nowhere Berel could hide.

She groaned at the complexity of the issue. In

the end, her only hope of happiness lay in Joseph still wanting her.

Berel looked at the tray, knowing she should eat. If only her body wasn't crawling in a mindless arousal, she would eat, but even roast kit and fried muklin couldn't tempt her. She panned her gaze over the tray, picking up the Gelgrin with a sigh. It wasn't the most nutritious choice available to her, but it was food that looked appetizing, and that was a step in the right direction.

It was a cloud in her mouth. Since Tirin's cook had shared his private recipe for the confection with Jole's, the palace had produced the finest Gelgrin on the planet. Berel closed her eyes, savoring the hint of lizor berry in the sucre and cream mixture.

She took another bite, her mind working on a new taste, a change the cooks had made in the confection. As a woman healer, there should have been no herb the cook could use that she couldn't identify, but Berel conceded defeat rapidly. Whatever it was, it was too faint to smell, almost too faint to taste, but it improved upon the flavor of the Gelgrin, which she'd thought impossible. She wished she had another of the confections. The flavor was intriguing...and she would love another chance to identify the herb or oil the cooks had added.

Berel curled onto her bed, abruptly dizzy. Her head ached in a combination of her pregnancy signs and her internal argument. She picked the lizor berry tea from the tray and sipped at it, noting that her mother had added just a few sand of olum to it today. As a woman healer, Syl wouldn't miss the fact that Berel was feeling poorly, and as such, there had been lizor berry tea on every tray she'd brought. The mug deposited back on the tray, she settled under the quilt, attempting to tune into her body's signs.

She furrowed her brow, cataloging her reactions in mounting confusion. Her skin was warming, her arousal mounting steadily. "Why is this happening?" she groaned. Joseph wasn't with her. He wasn't touching her. Why was she reacting as if he was?

Berel crossed her arms over her beaded nipples, her womb heavy and throbbing. She sobbed. She couldn't go to Joseph yet. Not until she knew how to approach him. Not until she knew what she intended to do if he didn't want her.

* * * *

Joseph looked up at the knock on his bedroom door, hooking his fingers behind his head with a smile. It was about time! "Enter," he called out.

His smile disappeared as Syl pushed the door wide and brought the tray of tea to his side. He lowered his hands to his lap, resisting the urge to fist them...or to scream out his anger. What would it take to convince Berel to come to him?

Syl passed a cup of redroot and implin tea into his hand.

"She ate the Gelgrin?" he asked.

"She did." Syl sat on the edge of the lounging

couch, offering him a weak smile.

Joseph laid his head back, sighing at yet another failure. "Why did you bring the tea?" he asked, reining in his frustration. "Why do you continue to let her hide?"

"Berel is not hiding," Syl countered.

"What do you call it then?"

She shrugged, a delicate hitch of her shoulders, almost careless. "Learning her place."

His breathing hitched. "You do know."

"Know? Know what, Joseph?"

Her confusion seemed sincere, but there was no way he could bargain that she'd chosen those words by coincidence. "What does Berel think her place is? Or mine?"

Syl's brow furrowed, and she scowled. "I have no idea. Her place is with you. Berel knows that."

"But she still refuses me."

"It will take time to—"

"There is no time!" Joseph calmed himself. "My apologies, Syl. I shouldn't take this out on you. In three days, Berel will be free to leave here, and the certainty that she is going to do that is maddening."

"She won't be leaving. You have my vow that I won't permit Berel to leave here in three days."

"What will you do? Use herbs to make it appear you're ill?" Joseph shifted uncomfortably at the thought of it. "I cannot ask you to do that."

If it wasn't for the problem of doctors being called in if he fell ill and discovering the deception, he'd suggest she give *him* a mild poison. But would his illness keep Berel with him? Not to mention, it would be more than a little dishonorable to play on her sympathies to win time with her.

Syl laughed heartily, touching Joseph's face as she had when he was a child. "Nothing like that, I assure you. And I will not make you ill, either," she chided him.

His face darkened. How well she knew him. "What will you do to keep her here?"

She turned her face away, her smile smug. "I have my ways, Joseph."

"Syl—"

"Now," she interrupted him. "What will you do tomorrow?"

Joseph stared at her. "What is the point? If the Dolgen didn't work—"

Syl looked back at him, her eyes glittering and her smile wide. "Only a bit of Dolgen. Gelgrin is so delicate that one cannot hide much of the oil in it."

"But it is the most powerful aphrodisiac in the world," he argued.

"Actually, it is not the most powerful."

Joseph sat forward, his breathing harsh in his own ears. If Dolgen wasn't the most powerful, why was he wasting his time with it and not pursuing her in the most expedient manner possible? "What is the most powerful? Will you teach me its uses? Why doesn't the book mention it? Why—" The questions burst forth without any sense of decorum.

Syl placed her fingers over his lips, shaking her head as if he was still a misbehaving toddler shouting out during one of his father's speeches. "You will learn that soon," she promised.

"Three days," he muttered.

"If it becomes necessary, I'll tell you everything you need to know before the three days are up. You have my vow...and you have my vow that Berel will not be leaving in three days. Now, what will you do tomorrow?"

He browsed the contents of the chapter in his memory. "The lizor freeze," he decided, seeking her approval of his choice. "At midday meal."

She chuckled at that. "An excellent choice. The touch of Garigol sap will relax her for the Dolgen's work." Syl kissed his forehead and rose, making her way to the door. "Sleep well, Joseph. Never doubt that Berel will be yours very soon."

Joseph nodded stiffly, wondering yet again what made Syl so certain that he'd convince her in the time he had.

"Oh, Joseph..."

"Yes?" he asked, half-lost in thought.

"Remember to honor Fion in your prayers tonight. Her gifts will bring Berel to you."

Joseph looked at the thick volume nestled between two law books in his library. *The woman healers were trained by Fion's Priestesses*, he reminded himself. "I will." *If it means a future with Berel, I will honor Fion every night of my life in the traditional fashion, kneeling before her flame in only my silin lounging pants, thanking her for her many blessings.*

CHAPTER TWENTY-⊕NE

Wos 7th, Ri 25-3010

Berel lay curled in bed, staring at the walls miserably. Everything around her made her think of Joseph and had for days. The imagined scent of him taunted her. Visions of them together plagued her dreams. Even sequestered in her rooms, she felt surrounded by him, and her body called for him endlessly. Of course, half of that would be the damned schen, but it shouldn't have been this powerful without Joseph close enough to influence her senses in other ways, more tangible ways.

There was only one thing left to do. She'd given her word, and it was the law. Still, Berel had refused Joseph; she'd hurt him. Worse, he hadn't attempted to contact her in the last five days. What if he didn't want her now?

She sighed. How long had she argued this? It seemed like she had for half the night. Berel was exhausted, but at least she'd come to a decision of how she'd proceed from here.

Despite the Trial Moon, Berel would not contract with a man who didn't want her. If Joseph didn't, she'd simply leave. It would be against the law, but better that than tied to a man who didn't want her, all for the sake of some ancient rite that should never have been drawn and used in the first place.

Berel looked at the clothing she'd packed, biting back a groan. She might have to finish packing, but it wouldn't be this morning. It wouldn't be before she knew for certain whether or not Joseph wanted her.

She pushed from the bed, resigned to her fate. Berel had to face Joseph today. He wouldn't expect to see her for two more days, but she couldn't put this off any longer.

Berel took her time, bathing and dressing in a woven gown that she usually wore when mixing herbs. If Joseph accepted her, there would be no illusions about what she was. She added a dab of the Cimmeg perfume and bound her hair into a thick braid down her back. With no further excuses to hold her there, she started off.

Her mother looked up from her inventory of stores, her herbs spread in the traditional pattern on the table. "Going to speak to Joseph?" she asked.

Berel blushed. "What makes you say that?"

Syl raised an eyebrow in censure. "You're miserable without him. Don't think I don't see it. Why in Len's name did you refuse him?"

She twisted at her bracelet, not meeting her mother's eyes. "Does it matter?"

"Maybe it does."

"Why would it?"

"Do you intend to let it continue?" she asked pointedly. "Are you going to let this push you further away from him?"

Berel shook her head. As long as Joseph wanted her, she didn't intend anything of the sort. If he didn't want her, it wouldn't be Corin and the other nobles pushing her from him but rather Joseph himself.

"Then why are you standing here talking to me?"

She shifted nervously. She was standing here, because it was yet another excuse not to face him. She was standing here, because she was terrified that she'd be packing the rest of her belongings in short order. If Berel confided *that* in her mother, Syl would repeat that she hadn't raised a coward. Worse, she might decide to stop Berel from following through with leaving the palace.

"Do you honestly think he'd refuse you?"

"Why not? He's not bound to—"

The open canister of dried Walla slipped from her fingers as Syl turned to her, her eyes hard. "You are *both* bound to contract, and you know it," she whispered fiercely.

"You..." Berel took a calming breath. Her mother had been a practicing royal woman healer for more than thirty years. Of course, she knew. Syl had probably recognized the signs before Berel had resigned herself to the truth.

"Of course, I knew. Did you honestly think you could hide something like this from me?"

"No, but..."

She stared at Berel, demanding an answer silently.

"No. I suppose I knew I couldn't," she conceded.

"Then there is no question of what you will do now, is there?"

"I won't use that," Berel insisted proudly. "He has to want me. If he feels he has to—"

"He's miserable."

Berel sucked in her breath in surprise.

"Joseph?"

Syl turned back to her work, brushing the Walla into the canister as if they discussed the weather and not Berel's hopes for a contract. "Who else? I hear he's been pining away, much as you have. He even called for a tea last night. I imagine he hoped I'd send you to him with it."

"Why didn't you?" Berel waited, barely breathing.

Her mother ignored her, stacking her canisters back into her emergency packs.

"Mother! Why didn't you?"

"You've created this mess. What would you have done at the end of the week? Would you have asked me to lie for you? I wouldn't have. You must know that."

"Of course not."

Syl nodded. "Then what would you have done? What do you plan to do, Berel?" she asked pointedly.

"If Joseph refuses me?"

She snorted as if in disbelief.

"I..." *Oh, what difference does it make?* No matter what, her mother would make sure she couldn't follow through now, whether she admitted her plan or not. "I won't be here. If Joseph refuses me, I will not be here two days from now."

"You have to tell him."

"No. I don't. If he doesn't want me without knowing it—"

"How do you intend to hide it? Honestly, Berel. You are more intelligent than this."

"I can't. Hugam is necessary, but I doubt

Joseph will feel the need to contract with me out of duty, either. Not then." *And perhaps he will realize how desperate I am to raise our child.*

Syl shook her head as if she thought Berel hopeless. "Go. Find him and talk to him."

Berel nodded, heading for the door.

"You are not leaving here without telling Joseph the truth. I will make sure of that."

"Then we will contract to the production of a child," she decided.

"You will sign the ritual contract."

"That is not your decision."

"Joseph and Jole will stand for nothing less than that."

"Then I will appeal to Susan. I will not accept payment for giving Joseph an heir. I can't do it."

Syl waved her toward the door. "As you wish."

Berel strode into the corridor and paused. She had no right to take the main stairs. There was no reason to. She turned right and took the servants' stairs to Joseph's rooms.

Her knock went unanswered. Berel looked around nervously. She couldn't just stand about and wait for him in the corridor, but she hesitated to make herself welcome in his rooms without his permission to.

Berel shook her head, furious with herself for her indecision. Though Joseph didn't know it, she had a right to be there. She was carrying his child under an unresolved Trial Moon; by law, she was already his bride. She entered the room, her head high.

His bed hadn't been made up. Berel looked at it, her heart aching. It was a weakness, the need to be near him. She sank to the bed and laid her head on his pillow, drawing in Joseph's scent. She gasped in surprise. Their mixed scent still marked his bed. A glimmer of hope lit in her breast. Had he requested the linens stay until there was no hope that he might win the contract?

Berel sobered. She was hoping for too much.

She stood, scanning the room slowly. There was only the bed or the lounging couch. The small desk wasn't a working space but rather a storage space; Joseph kept no chair at it. Berel turned to the couch, sinking to it with a prayer that their mixed scent didn't mark it as well. Her sanity wouldn't stand for that.

The truth was worse. The couch surrounded her in Joseph's scent, a much stronger scent than she'd expected to find, stronger even than the scent of the bed, as if... She looked at the bed, then sought out the quilt on the floor behind the couch. Surely, Joseph hadn't slept on the lounging couch for the five days she'd been gone.

Berel bit her lower lip, abruptly feeling as if she was spying on him. This wasn't right. She should leave.

No! I have to do this.

Not here. I could wait in his office. Being here is presumptuous.

Her heart skipped a beat at the sound of Joseph's voice in the corridor. Presumptuous or not, it was too late to leave.

"My office is there. If you'd be so kind as to wait."

Berel sighed in relief, glad that she'd chosen the bedroom—until he opened the door.

"It won't take..." Corin faltered as she spied Berel around Joseph's body.

Joseph was facing to the side, his head turned back toward Corin. He went still, perhaps reading the tension in the noblewoman he faced.

Berel held her breath as he turned, praying for a smile, for any sign that she was welcome. His shock was impossible to miss. Joseph looked at Corin, then back to Berel, seemingly at a loss for words for either of them.

Berel nodded. She stood, pretending to ignore Corin's look of triumph. Corin had the right to it; her prize was the greatest one Berel could imagine, the only one that mattered to her. Joseph had obviously made the choice his people would ultimately demand of him. Berel prepared for her first step toward the door, her back stiff and head high. She would leave, but she would leave with dignity.

"Leave us," Joseph whispered.

Berel met his eyes, swallowing hard to avoid sobbing aloud. She had no one to blame but herself, but she wouldn't give Corin the satisfaction of seeing her upset.

* * * *

Joseph shook his head, trying to discern the meaning of the pain in Berel's eyes. Understanding came with a pang of fear. She thought he wanted *her* to leave.

Berel nodded and headed for the door, accepting what she thought was his dismissal.

Joseph strode toward her, grasping Berel by the arms and bringing his mouth down on hers. She'd come to his rooms, and Joseph wasn't letting her leave until she came to her senses and contracted with him.

Her hesitancy crumbled in moments. Her responses were heated, passionate. Her hands traveled up his chest, and Joseph released her arms, skating his hands down her back to cup her closer to his rising erection. Berel moaned, clasping his head in her hands and pulling his mouth harder onto hers.

Joseph retreated slightly, lightheaded, panting in restraint. "Not you," he whispered his assurances. He turned to the doorway, glaring at his unwelcome guest while Berel pressed her cheek to his back, her arms wrapping around his waist. "I told you to leave us, Corin."

She blanched, motioning to his office. "I'll just wait for—"

"No. You won't. Leave." After that kiss, Berel wasn't leaving him, and he wasn't returning to his office for any reason today. He'd break laws to claim her, if it came to that.

Corin stormed into the corridor and shut the door forcefully, muttering curses.

Joseph stood for a moment, enjoying the feeling of her arms circling him again. Gods, how he'd missed this! He turned, and she released him.

Berel hugged her arms to her body, uncertain, unsettled. Was this what she'd been like the entire time they'd been apart? It hardly seemed possible, but he'd swear that her state was more pitiful than his own.

He stroked his fingertips along her lower lip, needing to touch her. "Why did you come here?" Why now? His planned doctored lunch tray was still more than an hour away. The Dolgen from the day before would have worn off during the night. Whatever drove Berel to him now, it was her and not some woman healer trickery. That thought warmed him.

She shook her head. "I had to... I—wanted..."

"Tell me what you want from me," he invited. Joseph sent up a volley of prayers to Fion that she'd come to ask for the contract she'd refused six days earlier. Even if she'd come to talk to him, to tell him what caused her to push him away, to give him the chance to resolve whatever problems she saw... Even that would be a blessing.

He'd been miserable without her. He'd barely slept or eaten, and the dark circles beneath her eyes and her pallor attested that she'd fared no better. How many prayers had he said, asking for this moment? Now she was here, and he was as powerless as ever to hold her if she demanded to leave.

"What do you want, Berel?" he asked again, terrified by her silence. "I will—"

"You," she breathed. "All of you."

An idea took shape. She'd come to his rooms and asked for all he had to give. Was this her way of saying she wanted the contract? Joseph refreshed his memory of the laws of Trial Moon frantically.

"Say it." If she said it—

Berel shook her head, trembling in his arms.

She started to pull away.

Joseph guided her to his chest. "Show me what you want."

She stopped struggling with him, nodding slowly. Berel unbuttoned his trousers and pulled his tunic up, the pads of her fingertips brushing over his stomach.

Thinking became a chore that quickly. "You want me undressed?" he rasped.

"Yes."

Joseph stripped off the rest of his clothing for her, dropping them to the floor. Berel paused, then pulled her dress over her head, holding it to her chest like a shield. He took it from her hands gently, tossing it as far away as he could. She kicked away her house shoes and took his hands.

Berel tugged at them, guiding Joseph to his bed when he complied. His heart pounded in anticipation. Joseph hadn't laid a single moment in the bed since Berel had refused him. Her scent had nearly driven him to madness, but he couldn't bear to lose that last tie to her.

She came to a halt, the mattress to the backs of her thighs. Joseph didn't give Berel a chance to freeze in indecision. He stepped toward her, pressing his body to hers—for an instant. She gasped in surprise, and he released one hand and turned, dropping onto the bed, gripping her other hand lightly, repeating a mantra in his mind.

Nothing she doesn't give a clear indication that she wants. Nothing...or this will fail.

Berel panned her gaze down his body, a look of longing on her face that made Joseph ache for her. She sank over him, proving the perfect match for him as she always had. Her body molded to his, the curves of hers finding the hollows of his.

Joseph fisted his hands in the quilt as she kissed him, reminding himself that Berel had to lead. The kiss progressed from tentative to fevered in a precious few heartbeats. She was like passion unleashed, and the temperature in the room seemed to jump markedly. He tangled his hands in her hair, unable to remain still when she enflamed him this way.

Berel pushed back, straddling his hips, meeting Joseph's eyes as if questioning his willingness to what she wanted of him. He nodded, urging her on. He ground his teeth as she seated him inside her.

Joseph grasped her hips, stilling her before she could take him in fully. "If you do this, I will finish," he warned her solemnly.

She nodded.

"You're a woman healer, Berel. You know what that means." *And she hasn't had enough time for Walla teas to be effective.*

"Yes. I know." She hesitated, her expression hopeful. "Is this what you want, Joseph?"

Her uncertainty confused him. Why was she here? What was she hoping for? "What do *you* want, Berel?"

"Everything. All of you, but..."

"But?" he prompted her. Did she have some demand she was afraid he wouldn't agree to? Considering the fact that he'd agree to almost anything she asked—

"Do you want me here? Do you still—want me?"

Joseph pulled her hips down to meet his thrust. Berel groaned and laid her chest to his, kissing at the base of his neck as he stroked into her again and again.

"I took you to Trial Moon, because I wanted everything, because I was determined to have you as my bride." *And the mother of my children.* "That hasn't changed. It will never change. I am going to take you to full completion." *And damned well do it right this time.*

Berel tugged at his shoulder, and Joseph took her hint and rolled her beneath him. He thrust deep inside her as he had the first time in his bed, a fierce mating, all-consuming.

She arched up, urging him on with a husky 'yes.' Her arms wrapped around his shoulders. "You still want me," she breathed, as if the thought amazed her.

"I will always want you. I want you to stay. Don't leave my bed today."

Her eyes closed, and she bit her lip, lost in pleasure. "Today?" Her voice was thick in near-climax.

"Today. Forever." *Either. Say either, but say it now.* "Will you stay?"

Berel's core spasmed around him. "Yes," she gasped. "I'll stay."

Joseph roared, losing his last tenuous hold on his control. His seed filled her; his cock swelled and locked into her stim band. Berel's eyes opened wide, and she pressed up as if seeking even more of him. For a long moment, they lay together in silence broken only by their ragged breathing.

He kissed her gently and smiled. She'd done it. She'd given him all the time he needed to convince her. "I call you to Trial Moon," he informed her.

Berel laughed long and hard, a joyous sound that he'd missed more than he'd ever realized he could. "You can't call me to Trial Moon."

"The forms were observed...again. There is no law that says I can't call you a second time."

She nipped at his chin playfully. "The forms were not observed," she assured him.

Joseph replayed their lovemaking frantically. "They were," he insisted, prepared to defend it to his father if he had to.

Berel shot him a smug smile and shook her head, running her fingers down his chest to the nest of their intertwined curls.

His erection lessened. "How?" he asked hopelessly. He had to know how she intended to escape a second Trial and plan his defense.

"The last Trial Moon lays unresolved," she whispered, her smile wavering. "You cannot begin a new one."

"Of course, I can." At the very least, he'd won himself the time to see if a cap formed from this encounter, another eight days. "All that was left was..." His breathing hitched at the possibility. There was one thing that would preclude him asking for a *new* Trial Moon. He looked between their bodies, then met her eyes. "Tell me," he pleaded.

Her expression was a heartbreaking cross between nervousness and fear. "Are you angry...or happy?"

"Please, tell me."

"You have an heir, Joseph." She tensed slightly, no doubt waiting for his reaction.

He laughed in relief, laying kisses on her face, cupping his hand beneath her navel. "Yes, I have an heir, but I have something sweeter than that."

"You do?"

"I believe so." He brushed his lips over hers. "Do I have you, Berel? Swear it to me."

"As long as you want me."

"Then you're never getting rid of me."

Joseph glanced at the bedside table, reality stealing his mirth. He laid a quick kiss on her lips and pushed off of the bed, pulling the quilt over her. In the blink of an eye, he was buttoning his trousers over his length again.

Berel watched him in what appeared to be misery. "What is it? What's wrong?"

"It's nearly time for midday, and I would wager you haven't eaten."

She blushed, reaching to pull the quilt back.

"Stay there," he ordered.

"I have to dress to go to the kitchen, Joseph... I mean... I suppose the dining room."

He marched back to the bed and tucked the quilt around her, his jaw tight in warning. "You will do no such thing," he informed her. "You promised not to leave my bed today, and a princess is bound by her word."

CHAPTER TWENTY-TWO

Berel smiled, watching Joseph close the door behind him. He'd left barefoot and bare-chested, heedless of the image he presented to the world. She ran her hands over her womb, wondering that she had ever doubted this outcome. How could she have believed Joseph wouldn't want her?

Her bladder beckoned, reminding Berel that there were some reasons for leaving Joseph's bed. She relieved herself and headed back, all too willing to let Joseph pamper her for the day as he wished.

She stopped at the desk, touching the iri bloom in a small vase in a mixture of happiness and confusion. It was a strange thing to see in a man's room when he hadn't expected a woman. A niggling of unease ate at her. Berel pushed it away. She had no doubts that Joseph hadn't invited Corin's attentions.

Then why the iri blossom?

She lifted the flower from the vase, bringing it to her nose and drawing the scent deep into her lungs. Berel gasped in understanding, recalling the flowers on her tray, almost every tray of food her mother had carried to her. There were always cuttings of iri.

"Mother," she spat. It really was beneath a woman healer to help Joseph trick her this way. There was no way Joseph had come up with the idea of painting his essence on the flowers alone. Even if he had, her mother would know his game.

There was no question that Syl had played along.

Berel replayed the days in her mind. All that time, she hadn't been imagining his scent; she'd been smelling him at his most potent. *Damn the man!* He'd set out to drive her mad, conspiring with her mother... Her face heated at that.

What other signs were there? Were there any? What else did he do? If he went that far, he probably went further than that.

"The Gelgrin," she whispered. What was the herb she couldn't identify in the Gelgrin?

Berel scanned his room with a critical eye. Where would he hide something?

She pressed her hand to the desktop then looked down, a smile curling her lips. Joseph was, first and foremost, a diplomat. He wouldn't dare keep something that would incriminate him in his office desk, but the desk in his rooms was another matter.

Berel pulled the deep drawer open, picking up the ancient woman healers' text with a nod of acceptance. So, Syl *had* helped Joseph plan this. This book was one that had been passed down in their family from at least the late Ri 24th era.

The containers of herbs and oils in the bottom of the drawer caught her attention. Berel pulled out a flask of Garigol. *Oh, yes. Only a woman healer would use crocks and flasks like...* She gasped, fingering the nick in the cap of the Garigol.

"Mother, how dare you!" Syl had taken these things from Berel's pack, knowing she wouldn't look for them until she left the palace. Joseph had used her own stores against her.

Berel pulled them out, cataloging what he'd done...or planned to do. There was dried lizor berry for calming. Joseph could have hidden that in almost anything without her noting the touch of flavor. In addition to the lizor teas, there were typically lizor freezes or jellies on her tray. "In anything," she muttered, setting the crock aside next to the flask of Garigol. Garigol was more difficult to hide. She was certain Joseph hadn't used the muscle relaxant yet.

She pulled out the final flask, staring at it in dismay. "Dolgen oil." That was what Joseph used in the Gelgrin. There was no doubt about it. The potent aphrodisiac would have caused the near madness for him that had plagued her all evening and her desperate need to see him that morning.

She sobered. No. Her schen would have caused most of that... The schen would have caused her need to see him today, at any rate. And it would have caused the bulk of her discomfort the night before. In the miniscule dose Joseph had given her, the Dolgen itself would only have aroused her long enough for a single encounter.

Berel flipped the book open to the blue silin marker, reading the chapter header in unease. In all the times she'd consulted this book, she'd never realized that there was such a chapter in it. How often would a woman healer play games like this with the lives of others? The thought unsettled her.

Joseph had pursued her in the only way left to him, using stealth and deceit to accomplish what she'd not permitted him to do any other way. Berel had been frightened by his failure to pursue her. Now she was angered that he *had* pursued her?

She sighed. Her mother had warned her that Fion would not permit people to run from Her gifts. Was it appropriate that Fion's knowledge had proven Berel's downfall? She conceded that it was.

Still, she owed Joseph return on his torture of her.

* * * *

Joseph pushed the door to his room open, his cock rising fast at the sight of Berel. She lounged against the pillows stacked at the headboard, nude, her legs folded under her and a book open on her lap. She lifted a flower to her nose and inhaled, raising an eyebrow to him in challenge.

He snapped his head around, looking at the open desk drawer, the smile fading from his face. Ice settled in his stomach, and his cock lessened.

Joseph looked at Berel fearfully. Would she denounce him? If she turned him over to his father, he'd lose her and their child, despite the Trial Moon.

He shook himself mentally. Without Berel, their child would be a bitter reminder of his greatest failure. No. If she turned him over for judgment, he'd relinquish the babe to her. Their child belonged with Berel, wherever that was.

"Joseph?" she prodded him, her voice and expression unreadable.

"I had no right," he apologized. He'd had no

right to read the missive sent to her. He'd had no right to pursue her when she'd refused him. "Berel, I know—"

"You're right. You had no right to do this to me." Berel motioned to the herbs and oils she'd set on the bedside table. "My mother helped you."

He winced. No doubt that hurt more than his deception.

"You used my own stores against me. Do you have any concept how...how appalling that is to a woman healer?"

"I didn't know that," he pleaded. "It's no excuse, I know, but I didn't know Syl gave me—"

"Put the tray down, Joseph."

He nodded, edging the flasks of oils aside to settle the tray on the table with them.

Berel met his eyes evenly, waiting but for what, he couldn't guess.

"Please, don't leave me." He prayed she'd let him explain and forgive him what he'd done. "I was desperate."

"By the laws of Trial Moon—"

Joseph grimaced at that. "If you don't want me," he began miserably.

Berel motioned him to silence. "Did I say I didn't want you?"

He shook his head, abruptly uncertain.

She stared at him for a moment then nodded curtly. "Neither will I allow such a thing to go unpunished."

Joseph took a deep breath with some difficulty, feeling as if a weight was sitting on his chest. "Should I call for my father?" he asked, his voice wooden.

"No. I think I'll know your measure soon enough."

"My measure?" Nothing she was saying made sense to him.

Berel nodded, flipping the page in the book and staring at it instead of him.

"I don't think I understand what you have in mind."

"Do you want me to contract with you?" she asked.

"On my life," he vowed.

She didn't reply to that. Berel plucked the lizor freeze from the tray and drank down a mouthful, trailing her opposite finger over a passage in the book. His eyes widened in understanding as she opened the flask of Dolgen oil.

"You're going to—"

"You used this knowledge against me," she noted. Berel poured a bit of oil in, giving it a stir with her fingertip.

Joseph clenched his jaw. He couldn't argue that point. "You're right," he conceded.

She held the glass out to him. Joseph hesitated only a moment before he took it and drank it down, grimacing in the certainty that she'd used more Dolgen oil than the book advised as much as at the flavor that he found hard to swallow. *At least she didn't use the Garigol.*

"Oh, perhaps I should have mixed that better," she commented, not sounding the least bit sorry that the Dolgen had settled to the top of the glass, a sucre sweet slug with an odd flavor he was unaccustomed to. At least the lizor freeze had cleared most of the taste from his mouth.

This isn't supposed to be pleasant. This was a punishment. Worse, it was a trial of some sort. Berel said she was taking his measure.

"Good," she said, taking the glass from his hand. She set the flask, book, and glass on the tray, meeting his eyes. "Lay down, Joseph. The effects will strike you soon."

He stretched out beside her. "What exactly is your test?" he asked, bracing himself for whatever insanity she intended to force him to.

"You ask me that now? Not before you drank the Dolgen but now?"

Joseph blushed. "I would do anything to keep you," he admitted. "If it means making a fool of myself—" He sucked in his breath as the throbbing settled in his length. It hardened, and he trembled in response. "What is the test?"

Berel turned onto her side and placed her fingertips to the pulse at his throat. "Mmmm," she purred. "Very good. Your pulse is elevated and your skin is warming. Yes, you're almost ready."

He was ready. The urge to pull Berel to his body and make love to her was nearly overpowering, but he knew that wasn't a punishment. "I'm not allowed to touch you," he guessed.

"You ruined my surprise."

She pressed her lips to his chest, and Joseph shivered in response. Berel unbuttoned his trousers, easing them off his body while the haze took hold of his mind.

The urge was maddening. He wanted to be inside her. He wanted to taste her. He wanted—

Her hand cupped him, and he groaned in response.

It wasn't enough. *Inside.* The need to be inside her was the only thing that mattered.

No! I will not fail this test.

Berel retreated with a chuckle. "Do you enjoy the sensation, Joseph?"

He shook his head, fisting his hands to rein in the need to grab her, hold her, claim her any way he had to.

"Oh? You don't like being aroused but unable to touch?"

"You could have come to me," he growled.

"It seems so simple to you," she mused, a flash of something sad settling in her eyes, then disappearing again. Before Joseph could question her, Berel continued. "There's something missing. Now what... Oh, yes."

She turned to her back, laying out flat on the bed, her hands caressing her stomach. His breath caught as she moved them up to cup her breasts...then lower, trailing lightly to the curls warming her mound. He forced himself to breathe.

Berel closed her eyes. Her back arched as she eased two fingers into her body. He groaned, rapt on the sight of Berel driving herself to release. His breathing was harsh, his control strained. Joseph's mouth watered. Gods! He wanted to drink her down and slide into her spasming body. This test was sure to drive him insane. As if in agreement, his cock pulsed toward her.

She moaned, her hips rising and falling, her breathing ragged, her head moving back and forth. Berel gasped his name, and he nearly gave in to the urge to pull her hand away and finish the job himself. She tensed, her body shuddering and her scent intensifying and changing to the sweet smell of her climax.

Joseph drew that scent into his lungs. "Let me make love to you," he pleaded. "I will give you whatever you wish, any pleasure you desire. I'll drink at your body, taste your lips—"

Berel's eyes opened. "What did you think of, Joseph?"

"Think—of?" Thinking anything was difficult.

"When you pleasured yourself to climax to paint the flowers every day? I thought of you stroking yourself. You did stroke yourself to climax, didn't you?"

He licked his lips. "Do you want to watch me?" he offered, praying she'd allow him self-release, at least.

"Oh, yes."

Joseph fisted his length, sighing at the slight easing of his arousal it brought. He worked himself.

Berel watched him, her eyes half-lidded. "What did you think of?" she whispered.

A plan unfolded in his mind. Joseph fought for clarity, for the ability not to be swept away when he wanted nothing more. *Almost nothing*, he corrected himself.

"You," he gasped. "So many images of you. So many touches." Joseph closed his eyes, reliving the weeks with her as his body neared completion.

"Tell me." Her voice came from just beside him, her breath heating his lips and her scent nearly sending him over on its own.

Joseph turned his head, feeling the heat of her lips close to his. If he moved slightly—

She moved away, no doubt anticipating the kiss he would have taken. It was probably better that he hadn't done it. He wasn't certain what she'd do if he didn't play by the rules she'd set.

"Tell me."

He sped his hand, his body reacting to the memories as much as to her voice. "You in the sea of flowers at sunrise, stunned by the colors and the sensations."

"And you."

He groaned at the knowledge that he affected her that way.

"And?" Berel prodded.

"You tending to Berisa, laughing with tears in your eyes, so happy that she lived."

"And grateful for your help in saving her."

"Your face at the height of the bel tro." Joseph cried out harshly, tightening his hand on the head of his cock as he erupted, his mind clearing as his body released in spasms that seemed to steal his will to move. His fist wasn't as comforting as her band, but it did the job...as he'd had to do the job every time he painted the iri blossoms for her.

Berel said nothing, letting his breathing smooth and his cock subside. She touched his cheek, and he nearly sobbed at the force and speed of his renewed arousal. Her scent on her fingers, compounding the effects of the Dolgen, was a lethal blow aimed at his libido.

"Self pleasure doesn't help, Joseph. I know." Her hands tended to him, cleaning the spilled fluids from his body with silin.

He swallowed his frustration, desperate for her to stop. The sensations were fast becoming unbearable. "You gave me too much," he breathed.

"I gave you little more than you gave me," she snapped. "The effects won't last long. I should have given you more."

"I understand, Berel. I apologize for using the musk and Dolgen. Please, stop this."

"You understand nothing—yet." Her hands became more purposeful, bringing him to aching readiness again.

"I wasn't touching you," he growled.

"You aren't in the throes of schen," she shouted.

Joseph forced his eyes open, horrified at the reminder. "Oh, gods. What have I done?"

Her scowl disappeared, replaced by shock. "Joseph?"

He touched the still-flat plane of her stomach. *Our child was within her, and I...* "I never considered. Mother Fion, forgive me."

Berel pressed her hand to his, her expression pained. "Dolgen oil is safe," she assured him. "Even Garigol, in small doses—"

Joseph winced. "But too much isn't. I know it isn't. I should never have used—"

"My mother knew I was carrying. She would never have let you use something dangerous to the babe."

"What if she hadn't known?" he argued. "What if I'd—"

"Joseph," she all-but shouted.

He looked at her, feeling sheepish. He was a Keen prince, trained for cool negotiation and battle, yet he was terrified. One threat to Berel and their child had him so scattered he wasn't thinking clearly.

And, he *was* thinking more clearly. Berel must have told the truth about how little Dolgen she'd given him. Already, its effects were fading.

Berel's expression softened. "I think you've been punished enough."

Before Joseph could question her meaning, she was over him, her mouth meshing with his and her hand guiding his still-hard cock to her core. Their mating was fierce, fast, and satisfying. In the aftermath, Joseph lay tangled with Berel, thanking Fion that she still seemed to want him.

He pulled the quilt over them, mindful of Berel's pregnancy signs. "Sign the contract," he begged.

Her voice was slow and sleepy, rumbling against his shoulder. "By the laws of Trial Moon—"

"Not that contract. Sign the one that my father's had locked away for three years."

Berel hesitated, playing her fingers in the curls between his male nipples. She nodded solemnly, not meeting his eyes.

"What is it?" he asked, suddenly wary.

"Nothing." She pressed her cheek to his chest, sighing. "There is nothing to be afraid of now."

Joseph wrapped his arms around her, his mind racing. How could anything have threatened Berel beneath his gaze? How could he miss something like that in his own home?

"What did you fear?" he asked, but Berel was already lost in slumber.

CHAPTER TWENTY-THREE

Ite 17th, Ri 25-3010

"Princess Berel," Radec of the Church Council announced.

The crowd roared its approval as the ceremonial crown settled onto her head. Joseph leaned forward and kissed her cheek.

Radec stepped to one side and laid the blue silin cloth over the bundle in Joseph's arms. He bowed his head and kissed the sleeping babe's brow, the only portion of him that Joseph had permitted to remain uncovered in the bitter cold. If it weren't for the fact that this was the heir to the Keen throne, he would have disappointed the assembled nobles and held the ceremony inside the ballroom.

"May you rule with Mag's justice and Fion's tender mercies," the cleric recited the ancient royal blessing. "May you serve your people well, as has your father before you." He nodded to Berel. "Name your husband's child, Princess."

Berel smiled at her husband and son. "I give you Joseph Hi The Younger, son of the heir apparent, Joseph Hi."

Radec shook his head at the strange Earth custom of naming first sons after their fathers, but he didn't comment. It was a mother's right to name her children, and though he would never have asked for it, she knew Joseph had longed for this honor.

"May you have many more," Radec blessed them solemnly, dismissing them to the warmth of the palace.

Joseph kissed her passionately.

Berel grasped his crown in one hand as it bumped with hers and slid away, a giggle bubbling into their kiss. She sent her husband an indulgent smile as she set it back on. "Behave," she whispered. "You've had me twice already today—once upon awakening, no less. Surely, you can't complain about a little wait."

Joseph brushed another kiss over her lips. "Anything that takes you from my bed after such a long fast had best be a planet-wide emergency."

"And you thought five days was hard," she teased.

"It was torture. Remember, I didn't know you were coming back," he groused. Joseph shifted their son onto one arm and used the other to guide her down the stairs and into the palace.

"Well," Berel sighed. "I suggest you get used to the idea of fasts."

Joseph shot her a look of dismay. "Why would I want to do that?"

Berel winced at the pure fear in his voice. She touched his cheek solemnly. "How many babies did you say you wanted?"

A rakish grin lit his face. "Ten," he teased.

She laughed heartily. "As you wish."

* * * *

"Joseph," Jenneane shouted, laughing as she

laid a kiss on his cheek.

He balanced the tray on one hand, snaking the other around her hip to steady her and the baby in the sling across her chest. His niece yawned widely, unaffected by her mother's outburst and sudden movement.

Joseph smiled at her. "I'm surprised Tirin let Rachel out of his sight," he noted, though he suspected highly that he hadn't.

Tirin was well on his way to being considered the most protective father on Kegin, a spot formerly held by cousin Alex The Elder. Joseph couldn't blame Jenneane's husband. After the fiasco of her search for a mate, no man would dare touch Rachel without leave to do so...now or when she was legally an adult.

Jenneane blushed, a clear indication that he'd been right about Tirin's ignorance of her current whereabouts.

Joseph chuckled. "You snuck away again. Didn't you?"

"I asked Panor to post a guard on us," she protested, motioning to the soldier standing a body-length away, his hand on the hilt of his blade and his gaze moving about in serious awareness of everything within striking distance of Jenneane.

Her blush darkened at Joseph's outright laugh. "And what kind of father will *you* be, when Berel grants you a daughter?" she challenged.

He didn't answer that, certain that he'd be just as protective as Tirin was. "Come with me. Tirin won't get too angry with you if you are with family."

They made their way across the crowded ballroom to the lounge where new mothers typically spent their presentation days, nursing and resting. Jenneane paused with her hand on the door, her brow furrowing in concern.

Joseph released her hip and reached past her. "Let—"

Jenneane clapped a hand over his mouth and shook her head, motioning to the door. Joseph handed the tray to his sister's guard and pushed the door open a crack in confusion.

"Listen," Jenneane mouthed.

Joseph pressed an ear to the opening as they had as children during the hiding game their mother called *Hide and Seek*. He covered his other ear, muting the sounds from the ballroom.

"It's not too late, you know. You can still save him from this."

He shot a startled look at Jenneane, noting her look of fury. She motioned to the door as if to convey a frustrated, "You see?" to him. What did she know that he didn't?

And...why couldn't Joseph place that voice? It was someone he knew though not someone he knew well.

Berel's reply was clipped and tense. "I think it's safe to say that I know Joseph better than you do. He has been born and raised as a Keen ruler. He does what he wishes, when he wishes, and a pack of sniveling nobles are the least of his worries."

Joseph scowled. What did the nobles have to do with this?

The other woman's voice took on a shrill tone

of warning. "You really believe that? You've heard it from more than my lips. The nobles won't support a lowborn on the throne. Prince Michael abdicated—"

"Because he wanted to," Berel insisted. "No one forced him to give up the throne."

"The nobles would have called for it. Someone like you isn't fit to—"

Joseph tensed, but Jenneane grasped his arm, shaking her head.

"Remember who wears the crown, Corin," Berel growled. "The Breeding Office sanctioned any match Joseph wanted to make. He chose me."

Corin laughed harshly. "The Breeding Office has no power. They proclaim Joseph's child royal for his father's re-bred genes. Don't flatter yourself that your involvement means anything. If you insist on this course, Joseph will have to step down—just as I told you long ago. You don't want that, do you?"

Berel didn't have a chance to answer. Joseph threw the doors wide open, his fury nearly blinding him. All he could see clearly was Berel's pale, strained face and his son feeding, while that carrion-eating bitch hovered over them.

Corin straightened as he turned to her. The urge to kill her was hard to quell. Jenneane's hand closed on his shoulder, granting him the calm he needed to speak.

"Get out," he growled.

Corin backed off a step in surprise, but she didn't retreat from his presence.

Jenneane's voice was no less threatening than his had been moments before. "If you are still here when Joseph holds my daughter, I will use his dagger on you myself." She reached into the sling as if to raise Rachel out.

Corin fled, stark terror in her eyes.

"Leave the tray," Joseph ordered the guard. "Then leave us." It was a sign of his upset that he didn't address the guard by name or rank, didn't take his eyes from Berel long enough to perform the most basic courtesies.

There was silence in the room for several heartbeats after the guard closed the door after him.

"Joseph?" Berel asked, not quite meeting his eyes...just as she hadn't met his eyes every time he'd tried to learn what she feared.

"This is why you refused me?"

She nodded, swallowing hard.

So many things Berel said made sense in light of this. It wasn't him that made her feel she was out of place at his side but the nobles. It wasn't him she was afraid of; rather, she was afraid *for* him. Most of all, Joseph understood why Berel argued his duty as if it couldn't include her, as if they had to follow separate paths.

"You—You thought I'd choose the throne over you?" Did she really think he was that shallow?

A tear ran down her cheek, but she didn't answer.

"Berel?" he prodded. "Did you think I'd choose the throne?"

"No," she admitted. "I thought you'd choose me."

"Then why would you refuse me?"

Berel looked at Jenneane as if seeking her

counsel.

"Talk to him," she suggested, lifting a squirming Rachel to her shoulder. "I told you from the beginning that Joseph had a right to know this was happening."

Joseph ground his teeth in frustration. There were just some things that were more important than a damned vow of secrecy. This should have been one of them.

Berel nodded. "I know you, Joseph. You love what you do, and you're good at it."

"What does that have to do—" he began angrily.

Jenneane smacked his arm. "*Shut up and let the woman speak,*" she ordered in the English that slipped out when she was ticked off.

Joseph nodded sheepishly and motioned for Berel to continue. He'd waited more than ten months to discover why Berel feared the contract so much. The least he could do was allow her to tell him the tale at her own speed.

"You would hate to give up your work. Part of me... I admit I fear that you would come to—to loathe giving up something you love so much...in time."

Yes, I would loathe it if I lost you, but it wouldn't take any time at all to come to that decision. He held his tongue. He had to let her say it all.

"But even more... Who would become king in your absence? Pyter? Gods protect Kegin!"

Joseph smiled at that.

"Gandl?" she continued in obvious distaste. "He wouldn't be half the king you would. Cro shows promise, but—" She seemed at a loss to explain her reservations. That wasn't unusual, when one was speaking about Cro.

"He has an odd way of handling people," Joseph noted. Cro made many people nervous. Some rumored that he'd inherited his father's madness. Joseph preferred to note that Cro simply anticipated people's reactions in a manner that made those around him uncomfortable.

He hesitated, considering Berel's fears. This upset wasn't healthy for her or their son. Worse, if she had enough of it, she might decide to dissolve the contract because of it.

Fury built in him. The nobles didn't control Joseph. Scaring off Berel wouldn't drive him to another woman, especially not to a grasping, conniving noblewoman like Corin.

There was only one way to handle this, and he had to do it now, before this stress destroyed Berel's ability to nurse their son and her confidence as a wife and mother with it.

* * * *

Berel lifted Joseph to her shoulder, burping him in the manner Susan had taught the woman healers would make human re-bred babies more comfortable. Her hands shook.

She cast nervous glances at Joseph, frightened by his silence and his fury. He held his body rigid. His eyes were dark and hard as if in decision.

Berel looked away from him, swallowing her

frustration, praying he hadn't chosen his duty. *He must make that choice eventually, but not today. If he must leave me, let him give me Joseph's nursing year. Give me that much time.*

But she wouldn't speak those words aloud. Berel wouldn't beg him to invest more time in a relationship he would have to abandon. Surely, Joseph realized that he must now.

She startled at the hands closing the nursing flap on her coronation dress, meeting Joseph's eyes. He knelt beside her, tying the bows, his expression pained.

Joseph took their son from her shoulder and cradled the babe to his own. He stood and offered her his hand. "Come with me."

It was an order, an order not unlike the moment when Joseph had ordered her not to leave his rooms. She nodded, placing her fate in his hands as she placed her hand in his and let him help her to her feet.

He took her arm but didn't speak. Joseph guided her through the ballroom and toward the entryway. As they came even with Panor, he leaned to whisper something in the security chief's ear.

Panor stepped back, shooting a look of surprise at Berel, then turning his face away. Berel followed his line of sight to the dais where the royal family sat.

"Now?" he asked, as if he were scandalized by what Joseph said.

"Now," Joseph insisted. "All of them."

"Your office?"

Joseph paused, glancing at Berel and away

again. "No. My father's."

Panor raised an eyebrow, but he kept his thoughts to himself. "Of course, Joseph." He made his way toward Jole and Susan, grasping several of his men along the way and giving orders as they moved. Those men nodded and headed off to the far corners of the ballroom.

Joseph didn't give Berel a chance to wonder at their actions—or to question them. He tugged her along with him, across the hall and into his father's office. Jenneane closed the door behind them. Joseph motioned his sister to Susan's usual chair then motioned Berel to the one beside it— Jole's place. She refused to sit, shaking her head frantically.

"Berel," he warned.

"It's your father's—"

"I know who typically sits there," he replied calmly.

"There are other places— *Your* seat—"

He guided her to the chair and motioned again. "They will all be occupied. Sit."

Berel hesitated, looking to Jenneane, hopelessly lost. Every ounce of training told her this was wrong. "Your brother is insane. You do know that, don't you?"

Jenneane chuckled. "You doubted that?"

Berel gaped at her, at a loss for words.

Joseph turned her so the chair brushed Berel's thighs. "Sit, Berel." It was a day for orders, it seemed.

She sighed, easing into the chair. Berel had no idea why Joseph was doing this to her, but it couldn't be good.

The door opened, and Susan strode in on Jole's arm. Berel winced, planting her hands on the desk to vacate his chair.

Joseph locked a hand on her shoulder. "Stay right where you are," he commanded.

Berel felt her face heat. She sent Jole an apologetic look.

Susan bit back a smile. "I assume there's a reason for this, Joseph?" she inquired in that oddly polite human way she still possessed.

"Absolutely," he answered, his voice tense.

Jole crossed his arms over his chest. "Would you care to enlighten us?"

Joseph's voice went deadly serious, cold and flat. "Not quite yet."

"When do you intend—"

The door opened again. Taven from the Breeding Office nodded to Joseph and Jole as he entered the room. Pyter and Gandl, together as usual, were right on his heels.

Berel watched in mounting dismay as Michael and Danellan, Cro, Ambassador Lian, Rebecca and Eve, Kyra and Diran, and almost a dozen heads of noble households squeezed into the office. It was no wonder Joseph chose not to use his own office. This crowd would have overflowed the smaller room.

She winced as Krynn from the Church Council followed Panor into the room. The security chief's nod cued Berel that the expected guests were all accounted for. She swallowed a sour wave at the sensation of being stared at by this forum.

Jole glanced around the crammed office, assessing Joseph's orders silently. "Well, Joseph.

This is quite an assortment of persons. Would you care to explain it now?"

Joseph didn't hesitate. "Jedal," he barked. "I had an interesting conversation with your daughter a few moments ago."

Berel bit back a groan as the lord flicked a look at her and darkened in some unnamed emotion.

"She told me," Jedal noted.

"Did she? Well, that's no surprise. I might have guessed that you were involved somehow. You agree with Corin's—mindset?"

Jedal slid an uneasy glance at Jole before meeting Joseph's eyes again. "I do," he admitted.

Jenneane made a sound of disgust at that.

"What mindset?" Jole asked, his eyes narrowing.

No one answered him. Joseph snorted. Berel ground her teeth, blinking back tears in the realization that it wasn't simply Corin and the other young nobles inciting trouble. If the heads of household were in on this, there was little chance Joseph would win the day.

"And the rest of you?" Joseph demanded.

Jole shot a hard look at the other lords. Berel's gut twisted at the lords' responses. They were discomfited. There wasn't a single face that lacked comprehension, that looked innocent of the plotting that had taken place.

"I see," Joseph mused. "Very well. You leave me no choice."

Berel buried her face in her hand, dreading the moment when he would make his choice public. Either way, Joseph was about to make powerful enemies—either his sisters or the nobles, by Berel's reckoning. Jenneane grasped Berel's free hand and squeezed in comfort.

"Joseph," his father warned. "Would you mind explaining..."

"Of course," Joseph snapped. "It seems that Lord Jedal and his co-conspirators have decided I've contracted with an unsuitable woman."

"They what?" Susan demanded, dropping her civil tone in favor of one that typically sent people scrambling to correct some grievous error.

"*Bastards,*" Eve cursed.

Berel snapped her head up in surprise at that, stifling a nervous laugh as the princess winked at her. Only Eve would dare say something so irreverent, and Panor flushed in exasperation with her in response. Berel bit her cheek to keep from laughing aloud at that.

"You had our word," Jole began calmly, and Berel's amusement fled with the reality of the situation.

"A king cannot rule without the support of the nobility," Joseph reminded his father. "You taught me that. You and Uncle Michael."

"Oh, no," Berel breathed, searching out Joseph's face. She'd never really considered what she'd do if he chose her. All this time, she'd secretly believed he'd choose the throne if faced with the choice, though she told herself otherwise. "You can't."

"I can, and I will."

"But, Joseph—"

"Will what?" Jole growled over her plea.

Joseph held Berel's gaze, patting their son's

back tenderly. "It seems your nobles want me to abdicate."

"No," Jedal protested. "We don't want you to step down."

"No," Joseph agreed. "You *want* me to give up my bride for you. Since that isn't going to happen while I live, the other option presented to me was abdication." A smile pulled at Joseph's lips. "But perhaps, I should make your choice clear to you."

He settled their sleeping son in Berel's arms with a kiss on her cheek. "For a few moments," he whispered.

"Clear?" Taven managed, looking decidedly ill.

"Clear," Joseph repeated. He stroked his fingers along Berel's lips and moved away, circling the desk.

Berel watched him breathlessly, the power that radiated off of him making her smile even in her terror of whatever game Joseph was playing.

Joseph laid a hand on Michael's shoulder as he passed him, nodding to his illustrious uncle. He stopped before his family, clasping both of Pyter's shoulders in his hands. "Guess who is heir if I abdicate?"

Pyter grinned. "Excellent," he cheered quietly, fisting his hand in victory.

Gandl rolled his eyes at the display.

Jedal choked as if he'd never considered the progression of heirs before. Or perhaps, it was simply Pyter's typical youthful disregard for decorum that grated with the old man.

Joseph skated his gaze over Jedal, then turned to Jenneane. "Of course, Pyter could abdicate or be deemed unworthy. Oh, big sister?"

he called sweetly, raising an eyebrow and waiting for her answer.

His twin laughed heartily. "As much as it would pain Tirin's mother to hear me say this, I wasn't made to be queen. You'll have to find someone else."

"*Fuck them,*" Eve shot at Jedal without waiting for Joseph to address her.

"Eve," Susan warned.

"This reeks of deceit, Mother," she protested.

"Much better. And yes—it most certainly does."

Joseph looked to Rebecca, leaving the question unasked.

She shook her head. "The women of this family have always stood together. I won't rule."

Joseph rubbed at his chin as if in deep consideration, ambling down the row of royals toward Michael's children. "The women always stand together. That is true. I should have seen that coming." He raised an eyebrow at Jedal and moved on. "Shouldn't I have seen that coming?"

Jenneane hid a smile behind her fist at that.

He stopped in front of Cro, leaning toward his cousin as if in commiseration. "If Pyter is deemed unworthy, you're next in line Cro."

The lords looked at the two men uneasily.

Cro smiled almost as widely as Pyter had a few moments earlier. "And you know as well as I do that I don't want the throne," he noted in obvious amusement.

Jedal let out a blast of air in relief at that pronouncement.

Joseph nodded, clapping Cro on the shoulder.

"Too bad. You'd make a good king," he complimented his cousin.

Gandl laughed harshly. "Which leaves me. I never thought I'd see this day."

"You still haven't," Pyter taunted. "I have to be deemed unworthy to hold the throne first."

"That won't be hard," Gandl managed, biting back a laugh.

Berel shook her head at their banter. Gandl and Pyter had always played well together, engaging in a friendly competition not unlike the one their fathers had engaged in.

Joseph nodded. "Well, it seems we have two willing candidates to take my place when I abdicate. I suppose I can do so without any qualms."

Pyter and Gandl stared at each other, their smiles faltering. As if communicating silently, they turned to Berel together.

Pyter shook his head. "I won't accept it. Not if I get it this way."

Jedal sighed in relief, no doubt thanking Mag he wouldn't have to find a reason to call for no confidence in Pyter.

Gandl shook his head. "I won't be a pawn to the nobles," he asserted. "If Joseph steps down, I do too."

Joseph cocked his head as if this move surprised him, though Berel was certain that it didn't.

He took two steps, bringing him even with Michael. "Perhaps we should send for Gibril," he suggested. "It would seem your eldest daughter is about to become the heir apparent, Michael."

Kyra laughed heartily at that. "Gibril doesn't want the throne. You can ask if you like, but I assure you that she prefers play to work. She finds politics tedious." She slid a sly look at Jedal. "And I'm never contracting. By Keen law, I can't inherit the throne."

Diran looked around, seemingly shocked. "Oh no, you don't. This is not being dropped in my lap. I serve in my own way."

Joseph bowed to her. "As you wish, cousin." He returned to Berel's side, facing the stunned lords fully again. "Well, this is very interesting. You gentlemen have a choice to make. Either Berel is your future queen, or you don't have an heir apparent. Which is it?"

Jedal sputtered, red faced. "You can't do this." He looked to Jole for a ruling. "They can't do this," he protested.

Jole smiled a smug smile. "They did. No law on Kegin says they have to rule. Come to think of it, no law says I have to rule either."

Jedal gasped at the threat left hanging between them.

Michael snorted in suppressed laughter.

Krynn cleared his throat. "The Church Council suggests you reconsider, Jedal."

Taven nodded furiously. "The Breeding Office granted any genetically-sound match Prince Joseph wished to make."

Lian furrowed his brow. "The Council of Worlds would strip our status for a coup of this magnitude. We'd be provisional for at least another ten years, all our trade agreements up for review and possibly forfeit. We'd have to prove our new government stable before we could even begin to rebuild what we'd lost."

"All very true," Joseph conceded softly, "but it would hardly be my problem. Would it, Lian?"

Lord Goren growled in displeasure. "Stand down, Jedal. We've lost. Admit it. You thought he'd retreat. He hasn't, and he won't, even if he destroys Kegin in the bargain."

Jedal shot a sour look at Berel that caused Joseph to fist the hilt of his dagger in warning. Berel and Jenneane each placed a hand on him to still him.

"What is your choice?" Joseph asked.

Jedal nodded. "Keep her."

"With your full support and blessing," Joseph demanded. "Your vow. All of you, and you will enforce that vow throughout your households."

One by one, the lords nodded their agreement.

Joseph lifted Berel's hand to his lips and kissed her knuckles, sending a tremor of awareness through her. It was a move that pronounced his protection of her, his possession of her, his tender feelings for her, and he did it in the face of his enemy in warning.

"Then you should leave and inform your people of our agreement. Oh—my dear nobles, one more thing."

They stared at him, suddenly wary.

"If anyone attempts to convince my bride to leave me again, she will tell me immediately, and that person will die in the traditional fashion. Jedal, your daughter has already had one escape. If she ever approaches my bride or children again, there won't be a warning."

Jedal darkened, but he nodded his understanding.

Joseph waved everyone away, offering Berel a smile that promised sensual delights to come. He leaned toward her and laid a kiss on her throat. "You need to relax," he whispered.

"And how will you relax me?" she questioned.

For an answer, he feathered his fingertip along the line of her hip. Berel gasped, nodding her agreement.

He stood and faced his assorted family, the only people who'd remained when Joseph had dismissed the nobles. "Thank you all for allowing me this."

Cro laughed. "That was an incredible chance you took. Gandl was sorely tempted, you know."

Gandl scowled. "If it wouldn't have made it appear that they could get away with the same with me," he grumbled. "I will be no one's plaything."

Joseph nodded. "I thank you for the sacrifice. I wouldn't have cared if you'd accepted the crown, but this works to all our favor."

Cro seemed deep in thought, his gaze traveling over Joseph and Berel. "You wouldn't have cared," he mused. "How intriguing."

Gandl nodded, heading for the door. "Next time, you're on your own," he warned. "I won't give up the throne twice in my lifetime." He breezed into the corridor without a backward glance.

Cro shook his head, watching his younger brother leave the room. "He'll never take the throne if the nobles have a hand in it," he assured Joseph. "Not now that he's tasted their games.

Ladies?" Cro moved between his sisters and offered each an arm, leading them back to the festivities.

Danellan threaded her arm through Michael's and settled her cheek on his shoulder. "That reminded me so much of the day you announced our contract to your father," she commented wistfully.

Michael chuckled, nodding to Joseph. "Well handled," he complimented his nephew. "If Cro is correct, and I never doubt that... If giving up what you'd hoped and trained for so long means nothing to you, you've found what's most important in your life." He glanced at his bride. "Never lose sight of the important things."

Rebecca waved a hand at them and followed Michael and Danellan out, Panor close at her heels.

Pyter offered a long-suffering sigh. "You could still abdicate," he suggested hopefully. "You'd have a lot more time to spend with your bride and children. I'd keep you on as an ambassador, of course. You *are* very good at your job, you—"

Joseph laughed aloud. "You'll have to come by the throne honestly, little brother."

Pyter glanced at their father's red-faced exasperation and shrugged. "You can't blame me for trying," he complained, ducking out of the room as Jole rolled his eyes.

Eve bit back a blast of laughter and started to follow him.

Susan cleared her throat. "We will discuss how you address nobles tonight," she warned.

Eve smiled. "As you wish, Mother."

She closed the door, leaving the last of the family behind.

Jole ran a hand over his mouth. "You could have warned me," he grumbled.

Joseph sighed. "You would have tried to talk me out of it."

"I would have ordered you not to do it this way."

"There was no better way," Joseph argued. "I had to end it now, and I had to make it clear that they could never try it again."

"And if someone would have called your bluff?" Jole asked pointedly.

"It was not a bluff."

Jole stared at him in disbelief.

Susan chuckled, guiding her husband toward the door. "I'll explain it to you," she offered. "Talk to him once you decide who you're really angry with."

Jenneane rose from her place at Berel's side. "I'll come with you. I think Joseph and Berel need time alone."

Tirin stormed through the door when she was halfway to it, looking irritated as he always did when she ducked her guards. "And just what were you doing this time?" he demanded.

Jenneane smiled sweetly. "Believe it or not, I just turned down the throne."

"You—" Tirin looked from Joseph to Jole and then back to his bride. "I don't... What did you..."

Jenneane placed Rachel in his hands and turned him toward the door. "I'll explain it to you," she repeated her mother's offer. "Then we can discuss my penalty."

Tirin's confusion melted into a hungry look that spoke volumes of his penalty for his wife's games of *Hide and Seek* with the guards.

Jole watched them leave in wonder. "She loves confusing him," he noted.

Susan sauntered ahead of him, stopping to cast Jole a look of invitation from the doorway. "All women do," she commented, turning away and leaving the office before Jole had a chance to recover his wits and follow.

Jole closed the door behind them, and Berel was abruptly aware that they were alone.

"And do you intend to confuse me?" Joseph quipped, raising an eyebrow.

Berel smiled. "I think we've had enough of that. Don't you?"

"I agree. We'll just have to agree to play games."

"Like the bel tro?" she asked.

"Not at all. The bel tro is a tradition, a rite of mating."

Berel met his eyes, taking stock of his playful smile. "Then what?"

Joseph leaned against his father's desk, shooting her a hungry look that put Tirin's to shame.

"No," she whispered. "Not on your father's desk."

"It won't be his desk forever," he reasoned.

"And *that* is when we will make love on it," she blurted out. Berel clapped her free hand over her mouth, blushing. "Dear Mag! What did I just promise you?" she exclaimed in a muffled voice.

Joseph laughed heartily. "I will hold you to

that, you know. A princess is bound by her word."

She lowered her hand. "So is a prince," she countered. "And you promised the bel tro."

He smiled, guiding her to her feet. "Hmmm... It is a tradition."

Berel stroked his rising cock through his trousers. "Joseph?"

"Yes?" he asked.

"It works, you know. Corin or no Corin, I would never dissolve our contract."

Epil⊕gue

Cored suppressed a shiver at the touch on his arm, wishing he'd closed off his senses. The woman touching him seethed in frustration and a wish for vengeance. If he wasn't in need of money, he'd brush her off now. Instead, he took a sip of the iri brandy in his glass and waited to see what she'd say.

He came to these functions for only four reasons. One was keeping his face known to his prospective mates and gauging their progress first hand. The second was keeping himself abreast of rumors that might aid him in his quest. The third was annoying his family with his continued existence and presence in their sacred circle...and the final was what this woman doubtless wanted. One couldn't make deals with noblewomen in rough inns. If one had wares to peddle, he had to go to where the clientele gathered.

"Cored Li?" Her voice was deceptively smooth, but he'd tasted the violence beneath her calm exterior.

"I am no longer a lord," he reminded her.

"No matter," she dismissed his comment.

Ah, but it does matter...to her and to every other noble.

Cored could feel her tension and dark amusement. She thought she was playing with him; little did she know that her games were wasted.

"And your name?" he inquired. Though he

would probably know her if he deigned to look at her, it would infuriate her that he pretended not to.

"Corin Laes, daughter of Jedal Li and Revi Laes."

Cored nodded. He'd heard the names many times. Jedal's family was one of the highest, and that meant deep pockets. It also meant that she was an ally of Cullin, and an ally of his brother's was no friend of Cored's. It was on the tip of his tongue to dismiss her, based on that alone.

Your plan! Remember your plan. The plan had to come first. To woo a re-bred, Cored would need items that cost much more money than he had. Corin's family could provide that money, and what better irony than allies of Cullin haplessly bringing him down?

"Of what service can I be to you, dear lady?" His tone was irreverent, his words ill-chosen...both choices befitting a rogue of his standing.

"I understand you stud genetically strong children," she replied bluntly.

"The highest levels of viability and vitality...if the gold is plentiful."

"It is. I assume the agreement you had with Gorun is sufficient?"

"Strictly speaking, my clients don't discuss our agreements." He sipped the brandy again, unwilling to commit to a figure until he knew for certain what Gorun had told Corin. Sometimes the esteemed *ladies* lied about their investments. That had worked in his favor before."

"When a woman pays two thousand gold per

month or portion of a month and another two thousand bonus for a daughter, she talks."

Cored smiled at that. Gorun actually paid three quarters that amount per month, though the bonus was correct. A pity he hadn't been able to collect that bonus and that she'd conceived in a matter of a few weeks. Sometimes he lamented that he was so fertile. Of course, much of that was due to the merciless way the noblewomen used him to get an heir quickly.

He sighed, raising the glass to his lips again. "I suppose she does," he conceded.

"Is the amount acceptable, or do I offer it to another?"

He stared into his drink, biting back the urge to laugh in her face. There were no other former lords possessed of the healing magic peddling their genetic code. If Corin intended to hire stud, it was Cored or a lowborn. Corin would never offer a lowborn even a quarter of that amount, even if she resigned herself to taking one to her bed...which was unlikely.

"It is acceptable. I will need to collect belongings from my home."

Including Dolgen tea. The *ladies* always wanted him often, to maximize their chance of conception within a reasonable time frame. If they were willing to give themselves to the mating, that wouldn't be a problem, but they didn't do that.

They invariably treated him like a mechanized sex toy, there to amuse them, to serve them. In their eyes, Cored was less than a slave, unfeeling, without needs beyond the bare minimum to survive, not to be trusted or even to be considered.

What man could perform under those circumstances without Dolgen?

He'd considered giving the Dolgen to his partner more than once. Perhaps that way, he would taste the true woman. He'd gladly take it as well, letting the aphrodisiac drive them through a night-long mating frenzy that would almost certainly result in a child, just to experience passion again.

Cored stiffened as Corin's hand stroked him, taking his measure behind the cover of her skirts. He scanned the crowd, ensuring that they were unseen, wrapping an arm around Corin's waist and guiding her into one of the deep alcoves that lovers favored.

"Very astute," she purred. "I've heard that about you."

"What else have you heard?" he countered, pressing her hand to his rigid cock.

"That you're a virile man who knows how to use his equipment."

"Then you've heard the truth."

He didn't question her intent. Ladies had played this game before. Cored slid a hand beneath her skirts, finding Corin slick and hot. He smiled. The idea of testing his prowess in a public place always excited them. In truth, it excited him as well. It was likely the most pure he'd ever taste Corin's arousal.

"There is a hundred coin bonus for this," he informed her. Cored didn't wait for her answer. He slid his fingers deep, capturing her cry in his mouth.

She pulled at his trousers, frantic as she

would probably never be for him again.

His cock ached in anticipation. How long had it been? Cored bit back a groan in the realization that he hadn't had sex in two months and hadn't had sex like this in over two years.

There were no words between them, no orders from the mistress who would dictate sex to him from this day until she conceived or sent him away. Cored thrust into her body, for one moment fully alive, the lord he was born to be and not a slave of his own making to reclaim his birthright, not an outcast in his own station.

Corin was fire in his hands, need without reason. He muted her scream of pleasure in his mouth, his cock locked tight in her body, the first of many times it would be.

She distanced herself slightly, her breathing harsh. Corin smoothed her hair, her abandon replaced with the cold, mercenary regard he hated from those bred to be hopefuls to the re-bred royals. "Acceptable," she noted. "My coin may be well spent, after all."

Cored forced his jaw to unlock, the memory of Cullin talking and laughing with Prince Joseph stilling his drive to walk away from Corin this moment, plan or no, vengeance or no.

"I will expect you at my retreat home in Berenal in the morning," she continued.

"As you wish," he managed through gritted teeth. *But not forever. Someday, I will claim a re-bred bride.*

The End

About the Author

Brenna Lyons wears many hats, sometimes all on the same day: former president of EPIC, author of more than 100 published works, owner of Fireborn Publishing, columnist, special needs teacher, wife, mother...and member in good standing of more than 60 writing advocacy groups.

In her first ten years published in novel-length, she's won 3 EPIC e-Book Awards (out of 15 finalists) and finaled for 3 PEARLS (including one Honorable Mention, second to NY Times Bestseller Angela Knight), 2 CAPAS, and a Dream Realm Award. She's also taken Spinetingler's Book of the Year for 2007.

Brenna writes in 26 established worlds plus stand-alones, poetry, articles and essays. She's a bestseller in indie/e fantasy and horror, straight genre and cross-genres thereof. Brenna has been termed "one of the most deviant erotic minds in the publishing world...not for the weak." (Rachelle for Fallen Angels Reviews) Milieu-heavy dark work is practically Brenna's calling card, with or without the erotic content.

She teaches classes in everything from POV studies to advanced editing, networking to marketing. Brenna enjoys hearing from people who read her work and can be reached by e-mail.

Website: http://www.brennalyons.com/

Facebook: http://www.facebook.com/brenna.lyons

Email: brennalyons4168@live.com

ALSO BY THIS AUTHOR

The Master's Lover

DAN AIDAN FAIRIES
Fairy Dreams
Monsters of Myth Anthology

XXAN WAR
Daahan Rising
Raashh Decisions

MYTHOS SERIES
The Punishment of Phoebus Apollo
Black Sail

IT'S ALL GREEK TO ME...
All's Fair...

SANCTUM
Dream Walk

GRELLAN WAR
With Great Power

BLOOD MAGES
Enslaved

CARSON COUSINS
All I Want for Christmas is You

FATES WAR
Fates Magic

Beyond the Veil
Mine for the Night
Once in a Blue Moon
Overtime Pay
Stay With Me
The Fire God's Woman
Nevermore
Bride Ball
Undead in Blue

Mama's Tales
Unexpected Daddy
We Shall Live Again
May the Best Man Win
Marked
And It Was Good
Monsters of Myth Anthology

Available from **Under The Moon**

Evil Overlords Union Issue #1 Anthology
Undead Embrace
"Playing Games" in *Forbidden Love: Bad Boys*
"Marked" in *Forbidden Love: Wicked Women*
"The Master's Lover" in *Forbidden Love: Sacred Bands*

Available from **Logical Lust**

"Mine for the Night" in *The Cougar Book* Anthology

Available from **Coming Together Charity Anthologies**

INSTINCT SERIES
"Foundling" in *Coming Together: Into the Light* Anthology

"Claim Mate" (available separately and as part of the
Coming Together: Against the Odds Anthology)
"The Fire God's Woman" in *Coming Together: Under Fire*
Anthology

Available **self-published**

Snapshots from a Poet's Life

Award-Winning Books

EPPIE/EPIC eBOOK AWARDS WINNERS
Coming Together: Against the Odds- 2010
Time Currents- 2010
Coming Together: Into the Light- 2011

EPPIE/EPIC eBOOK AWARDS FINALISTS
Fion's Daughter- 2004
Collected Poems: Book One- 2005 (now titled *Snapshots of a Poet's Life*)
Renegade's Run- 2005
Rites of Mating- 2006
All I Want for Christmas- 2006
Phaze in Verse- 2008
"The Fire God's Woman" in *Coming Together: Under Fire*- 2009
Three Wishes- 2010
Matchmaker's Misery- 2010
The Cougar Book- 2011
The Master's Lover- 2011
Bride Ball- 2011

DREAM REALM AWARDS FINALIST
Last Chance for Love- 2003

PEARL HONORABLE MENTION
Night Warriors- 2004

PEARL FINALISTS
Schente Night- 2003 (now included in *The Last of Fion's Daughters*)
König Cursebreakers- 2004 (now titled *Will of the Stone*)

JOYFULLY REVIEWED BEST BOOKS OF 2010
Written in the Stars- 2010

SPINETINGLER'S BOOK OF THE YEAR 2007

NOBODY: An Anthology of Dark Fiction- 2007 (Brenna's pieces of the anthology can be found in *Beyond the Veil*)

TRS's CAPA FINALISTS
Ultimate Warriors- 2004 (Brenna's portion is now available as *With Great Power*)
Written in the Stars

LOVE ROMANCE AND MORE CAFÉ BOOK OF THE YEAR RUNNER UP
Last Chance for Love- 2008

ROAD TO ROMANCE REVIEWERS' CHOICE AWARD
Prophecy: Revelations- 2004

LOVE ROMANCES REVIEWERS' CHOICE AWARD
Black Sail- 2003

ROMANCE JUNKIES BOOK CLUB STAFF PICK
TYGERS- 2003

FALLEN ANGELS ROMANCE RECOMMENDED READ
Devon's Price-2005 (now available in *Bearing Armen*)

JOYFULLY RECOMMENDED READ
Fairy Dreams- 2008
The Last of Fion's Daughters- 2009

TREBLE HEART FINALIST
Prophecy: Revelations- 2003